DISTANT SUN

When, unexpectedly, a free cruise down the Nile is offered to Cathy she thinks it's the answer to her holiday problems. All she has to do is see if there is any way of improving the experience . . . Instead, she finds herself in danger from unknown enemies who will stop at nothing to get what they want. How can she tell friend from foe? Who can she trust? And romance with a charming stranger makes Cathy's life even more complicated . . .

SHEILA HOLROYD

DISTANT
SUN

Complete and Unabridged

LINFORD
Leicester

First published in Great Britain in 2009

First Linford Edition
published 2009

British Library CIP Data

Holroyd, Sheila.
    Distant sun. - - (Linford romance library)
    1. Cruise ships- -Nile River- -Fiction.
    2. Romantic suspense novels.
    3. Large type books.
    I. Title II. Series
    823.9′2–dc22

ISBN 978–1–84782–905–4

Published by
F. A. Thorpe (Publishing)
Anstey, Leicestershire

Set by Words & Graphics Ltd.
Anstey, Leicestershire
Printed and bound in Great Britain by
T. J. International Ltd., Padstow, Cornwall

This book is printed on acid-free paper

1

'No, I quite understand,' Cathy Singleton said calmly. 'Don't worry about me. I'll see you when you get back.'

She replaced the telephone receiver gently, then closed her eyes, clenched her fists, took a deep breath, and thumped her desk hard. Feeling a little better, she opened her eyes and saw the owner of the travel agency, John Hunter, standing in front of her with his eyebrows raised.

'What's wrong?' he said with interest. 'If you like, you can scream out loud. Just give me warning.'

Cathy managed a weak smile.

'My holiday plans have just been ruined. Next week I was going walking in the Lake District with Mary, and now she's just called to say that her boyfriend has booked a surprise week in Majorca for the two of them and she's sure I will understand that she would rather be with him.'

'And do you?'

Cathy shrugged.

'Of course, Majorca does sound a lot more glamorous, especially with a boyfriend.' She bit her lip. 'But walking up the hills by yourself is a bit lonely, and I booked double rooms, of course, so now I'll have to pay extra . . . '

'And the weather forecast for Cumbria is absolutely dreadful,' John Hunter informed her. 'In fact, Cathy, I think you should forget about the Lake District. Treat yourself. Someone has just had to cancel a holiday in Egypt, flying from Heathrow on Sunday. I'll let you have it at cost price.'

Cathy looked at him with sudden deep suspicion.

'Why?'

He looked hurt.

'Because I'm sorry for you, because your holiday plans have been ruined.'

'Not good enough. You are not given to fits of generosity.'

John Hunter tried to look even more hurt, then gave up the attempt and grinned.

'All right. I've been thinking for some time that we ought to check up on our Egyptian holidays. Someone like me who is known to be a travel agent is treated like royalty by hotels and cruise boats, but if you went as an ordinary tourist you could see how well they treat our ordinary customers and whether there is anything we should alter.'

Cathy gazed at him stonily.

'So actually you are not offering me a holiday. You want me to spend my time making notes and dreaming up suggestions. And you expect me to pay for it!'

'All you have to do is behave like an ordinary holidaymaker for most of the time. Just jot down anything you notice that you think is particularly good or bad. It won't take more than five minutes a day so I did think you might contribute a little towards the cost. Now, what do you say?'

'No,' Cathy said firmly.

John Hunter looked at her in disbelief.

'Cathy Singleton, instead of a rain-soaked lonely tramp through the Lake District, I am offering you a luxury holiday in one of the most fascinating places in the world. Why won't you go?'

Cathy shuffled uneasily, avoided his eyes and gazed down at her desk.

'Because I would have to fly and so far I've managed to avoid that.'

Now he was really fascinated and leaned forward across the desk.

'Do you mean you have never flown? But you are twenty-four, or is it twenty-five? I thought everybody in England started flying before their teens nowadays.'

'My family always went on camping holidays in England. Now my parents have a caravan in Devon and I usually go hiking or exploring part of Britain.' She drew herself up. 'I'm not really scared of flying, just a little apprehensive, and I need more than a few days to prepare myself. Incidentally, I'm twenty-three!'

John Hunter waved away her protestations.

'The less time you have to prepare, the better. In fact, if it were possible, I'd drag you off for a flight this afternoon. Come on, Cathy, I'm offering you a great opportunity.'

'I don't want to go.'

'You are scared.'

'No!'

She glared at him and he patted her hand soothingly.

'Look, Cathy, you have been working for me for just over a year and you are good at your job. I think you are ambitious and you could do well in the travel industry, but inevitably that will involve flying sooner or later.'

She did not respond, and her boss sighed and went on. 'Think of Mary lying in the sun in Majorca while you slosh through the mud. Next time you see her, wouldn't you like to be able to tell her that you have been on a wonderful holiday in Egypt?' He saw Cathy blink and went on persuasively. 'You'll sail down the Nile on a five-star cruise ship and then stay in a luxury hotel in Luxor. Think how jealous she will be.'

Cathy looked at her boss bitterly.

'You're playing dirty.'

'Of course. But will you go?'

She frowned, tapping her fingers on the desk, then looked up suddenly.

'All right, I'll go — on condition I don't have to pay anything.'

John Hunter smiled broadly.

'Done! I'll give you all the details and we'll get the tickets sorted. I suppose you have got a passport?'

'Yes. I went to France a couple of years ago for a walking holiday.'

'Then there are no problems. You know what the brochures say anyway, but I've got a couple of books on Egypt you can look through. Don't forget to order some Egyptian money from your bank. I may be giving you a free holiday, but I'm not giving you your

6

pocket money as well.'

He stood up, obviously well satisfied.

'Do you know,' he said, 'I'm quite grateful to Mary.'

Once he had gone, Cathy began to regret her decision, but it was too late to change her mind without looking extremely foolish. Anyway, she knew that it would indeed be a holiday to remember. Hunter's Tours was a small firm with a high reputation for attention to detail and personal service. It organised package holidays aimed at the older, well-to-do traveller, as well as bespoke holidays for the seriously rich, and Egypt was a favourite destination. Cathy had often wondered what it would be like to go there if only she didn't have to get there in an aeroplane!

The next few days were too full for her to have any time to worry. Even in May Egypt would be hot, so she rushed round the nearby shops and bought loose, lightweight clothes that could be drip-dried in a bathroom. Her mother came home from a shopping trip laden with high-factor sun cream, insect repellent, and pills for stomach upsets as well as headaches.

'Eat lots of yoghurt!' she advised her daughter. 'Everybody says that helps you avoid tummy bugs.'

Early on Sunday morning, having made her check three times that she had all the necessary documents, her parents drove her to Heathrow. They helped her find out the number of her check-in desk and insisted on accompanying her until she was safely checked in and had entrusted her luggage to the airline. She finally said goodbye to them as she went through into the departure lounge, turning to wave until she could no longer see them.

In the departure lounge Cathy found an empty seat and sat down suddenly feeling very lonely, and she hurried to the departure gate as soon as the notice came up. After half an hour fidgeting on an uncomfortable chair she was glad to be ushered along a silvery metal tunnel into the aeroplane. Soon she was settled in a window seat, her safety belt tightly fastened. Then, suddenly, the roar of the engines filled the cabin and she grew tense and apprehensive. Vaguely she was aware of someone sitting down in the empty seat beside her, but at that moment the plane began to move and she shut her eyes tightly. It moved faster, and she gave a little moan.

Unexpectedly she felt a warm hand enveloping hers.

'Your first flight?' said a voice beside her. 'Just relax. Hold my hand if you like.'

Like a child, she seized the stranger's hand as the plane rumbled along. Then the noise lessened and she suddenly felt lighter.

'We've taken off. Why don't you have a look?' said the voice.

Slowly Cathy opened her eyes and risked a quick glance out of the window. She stared, and then craned her head to look at the panorama beneath them, at the clusters of houses and the patterns of fields, marvelling at the tiny cars crawling along the road like an animated map.

'Could I have my hand back now?' said a voice a little apologetically, and Cathy turned from the fascinating spectacle below to the man sitting beside her. He was in his thirties and his black curly hair and deep tan gave him the look of a gypsy, an appearance contradicted by his grey business suit. She released her grip and he began flexing his hand carefully.

'I'm sorry. I didn't mean to hurt you,' she apologised.

He managed a smile, and she saw that he had dark grey eyes with enviably long lashes.

'I don't think there is any permanent damage,' he said carefully.

At that moment the cabin darkened and Cathy clutched his arm.

'It's all right. We are just flying through the cloud layer,' he assured her patiently, and at that moment the plane burst through into brilliant sunshine over a fluffy white carpet of cloud.

'Amazing, isn't it?' said her companion. 'Every time there is a really miserable day I cheer myself up by thinking of the sun above the clouds.'

Cathy nodded, still looking out the window. Then, miraculously, the clouds vanished and she was looking down at the sea where tiny boats were visible far below.

The flight was without incident and her companion was content to leave her to stare out at Europe passing beneath them. The snow-capped mountains of the Alps held her spellbound. Then it was the blue waters of the Mediterranean, and then they were flying over bare desert, arid desert.

'It isn't long till Luxor now,' said the man beside her. 'Have you enjoyed your first flight after all?'

'It's been wonderful!' Cathy said sincerely. 'I don't know why I was so nervous.'

But she began to feel a little worried when the pilot announced that they would soon be landing. Wasn't that a more difficult manoeuvre than taking off? She began to fidget.

'All right, here's my hand,' his voice said resignedly, and she was grateful for the comfort his warm grasp gave her for the short time it took the plane to land smoothly. She lost sight of her neighbour as she followed the other passengers out of the plane and reproached herself for not thanking him.

Outside, hot, dry warmth surrounded her, and the sunlight had an unusual clarity.

Dusk was already beginning to fall when the minibus carrying Cathy and a dozen other travellers reached the riverbank and they crossed a short gangplank into their boat. Cathy had a confused impression of shining brass and polished wood before a smiling steward showed her to her cabin.

When the door shut behind him Cathy gave a sigh of relief, kicked off her shoes, lay down on the bed and closed her eyes. The anxiety she had been feeling for the past few days had vanished. She had completed her first flight in an aeroplane and now she was in Egypt, ready to enjoy a five-star holiday at her firm's expense.

After a while she sat up and looked around, and her eyes widened. Her cabin was like a luxurious hotel room and the spacious bathroom was quite unlike the little cubicles she was used to on holiday. She went to the window and opened the heavy curtains. Outside the Nile glimmered as the sun sank lower in the sky. On the far bank there were tall palms. She stared. Yes! There was a camel swaying along the road by the riverbank!

With an hour to go before dinner, Cathy showered and then spent some time hanging up her clothes and wondering what people wore in the evenings on board before she finally settled on a pretty summer dress. It was several hours now since she had eaten on the plane and she was feeling hungry, but when she heard a gong being struck she felt uncertain and unready. She was about to meet the people with whom she would spend the next few days and in a way she would be spying on them.

'Hunter's Tours?' she was asked, and was ushered to a table for eight. Cathy knew that most Nile cruisers usually carried several groups, and as she looked round she could hear Italian and French being spoken. The tables that had been reserved for Hunter's Tours gradually filled up and Cathy's spirits fell just a little.

Her fellow travellers were, to say the least, mature. Some were probably celebrating recent retirement, but others looked as if they might have been present when Tutankhamun's tomb was opened in the nineteen-twenties. Six people took their seats at her table and greeted her politely, each of them clearly examining the other diners with covert curiosity and wondering whether they would be agreeable travelling companions or absolute pests. Anyway, Cathy decided she had chosen the right thing to wear, which was a relief.

One woman had obviously been up the Nile before and was already giving advice to the others.

'Don't give anything to a child!' she said firmly. 'Give one of them a sweet, for example, and suddenly a dozen others will appear, all wanting sweets.'

Cathy listened anxiously, and then realised that the last seat at the table was being taken. She turned to smile at the newcomer, and recognised the dark hair and tanned face.

'Hello!'

'We meet again,' he said politely.

The rest of the table was obviously interested, and the man flashed a quick smile at the other diners.

'This lady and I met on the flight from England,' he announced. 'My name is Tom Sanderson, by the way.'

'Where did you get to? You weren't on the coach,' Cathy asked Tom.

'I had to call in somewhere on the way so I took a taxi. What do you think of the boat?'

'I'm very impressed so far,' she replied, and did not realise till after how deftly he had changed the subject.

One of the women at the table, whose blonde hair and sun dress were rather too youthful for her mature years, introduced herself as Mavis Elton.

'When you have travelled as much as I have — and I always go five-star, of course — you won't be so easily satisfied, my dear.' She proceeded to give a list of petty complaints about the boat.

The lady who had been giving advice to the others earlier, and who was called Mrs Redcar, cut her off crisply.

'Well, my experience is also extensive, and I like the boat.' She looked at Cathy and Tom with curiosity. 'If you don't mind me saying so,' she said in a tone which made it clear that she did not care if they minded or not, 'you two aren't like the usual Hunter's Tours clients. They don't often get young people travelling alone with them.'

'I'm here half for pleasure and half on business,' Tom Sanderson replied without hesitation. 'I had to come and see some people in Egypt and I found I could combine it with the cruise, so I am enjoying the best of both worlds. A cruise is a great way to get between meetings. What about you, Miss Singleton?'

Cathy had her cover story ready.

'I work for a firm which organises conferences. Summer is their busiest time, so they prefer me to take my holidays early.'

'Organising conferences seems to be a growing business. What exactly do you do?'

'Oh, I just work in the office, collating information and dealing with correspondence.'

Cathy had thought this would be enough to satisfy enquiries, but she had underestimated Mrs Redcar's ruthless directness.

'You work in the office? I shouldn't have thought you earned enough there to pay Hunter's Tours prices.'

Cathy thought quickly.

'I'm afraid that's true, but fortunately I got lucky with a scratch card and decided to treat myself.'

There was a rustle of interest and one man was eager to tell the story of a fortunate bet on a horse while even Mrs Redcar didn't feel she could ask Cathy bluntly how much she had won, so the conversation gradually developed into a discussion on travel which lasted for the duration of a very pleasant meal.

Although Tom gave no more information about himself, the other diners were eager to talk about their experiences and seemed to have covered the world between them. They were amazed when Cathy confessed that a short trip to France had been her only travel outside Britain so far.

'You'll love Egypt,' one man told her earnestly. 'You'll want to come back. This is our fifth cruise up the Nile.'

Coffee was served in the lounge, where promptly at nine-thirty Magid, who had introduced himself as their guide, gathered his little flock together and explained that the boat would sail to Aswan overnight and that they would start their first visit to a temple early in the morning so as to avoid the worst of the heat.

'Don't worry about being late for breakfast. You will get a wake-up call,' he assured them. 'Now, you've all travelled a long way today and you have a lot to see tomorrow. May I suggest you have an early night? Sleep well!'

Most of them obediently stood up and began to make their way to their cabins. Cathy found herself going in the same direction as Mrs Redcar.

'I like your boyfriend,' Mrs Redcar commented.

'My boyfriend? If you mean Mr Sanderson, I only met him today!'

'I'm talking about the future,' the lady said enigmatically. 'Goodnight.'

Inside her cabin Cathy suddenly felt very tired. It had been a long, full day and she was too weary to make any notes for John Hunter or to think about Tom Sanderson. Quickly she washed and tumbled into bed and fell fast asleep, only waking briefly in the middle of the night to hear the soothing purr of the engines as the boat made its way upstream.

2

'It is six-thirty. This is your wake-up call,' the voice said brightly. Cathy mumbled something unintelligible and managed to put the receiver back on the phone on the bedside table

Six-thirty in the morning and she was supposed to get up? She levered herself into a sitting position and glared round the cabin. She didn't even get up at that early hour when she had to get to work, and now she was supposed to be on holiday!

Reluctantly she climbed out of bed and made for the bathroom. A quick shower woke her enough to dress in jeans and a T-shirt and comb her hair, then she made for the restaurant where she found other holiday-makers similarly tired and disgruntled. Mavis was denouncing the early start as completely unnecessary. Strong coffee and orange juice helped Cathy's state of mind and she managed to nibble a piece of toast. Then she remembered her mother's advice and dutifully ate a yoghurt.

'Good morning,' someone said far too briskly. Mrs Redcar, neatly dressed and with every hair in place, was enjoying a full breakfast.

'Do we really need to get up at this hour?' Cathy complained.

'This isn't early! Wait till you get up at four to see the sun rise and go hot-air ballooning.'

'I may skip that,' Cathy said with deep feeling.

A few hours later she was exhausted, sunburnt, footsore, and madly in love with Egypt. She had seen two-thousand-year-old temples and modern marvels of engineering, admired intricate works of art and all the time she had been aware of the blue sky overhead and the sun shining down on golden stone. Now her head was a whirl of sound and colour and exotic names. She was guiltily aware that some of the confusion was her own fault because she had not made time during the previous few days to look through a guidebook. As a result, although Magid's explanations were very clear, she had soon lost track of the pantheon of Egyptian gods, not sure of the difference between Hathor and Horus.

However, she had not realised that each ancient site was accompanied by a large outdoor market, and nothing could have prepared her for full force of the Egyptian stallholders' belief that all tourists needed souvenirs of many kinds, from gaily embroidered robes to dubious antiques and countless busts of Tutenkhamun, and that these souvenirs should be bought from them.

They clamoured to the sightseers to come and buy, holding out their wares and praising them to the skies. Cathy was attracted by a soft white cotton scarf, which she thought would shield her neck and shoulders from the sun. The stallholder saw her looking at the scarf and thrust it at her.

'How much?' she asked, and the seller named a surprisingly high price. She shook her head and started to move away, but he moved into her path, still holding out the scarf. Mrs Redcar came to the rescue.

'Offer him half as much,' she commanded. Cathy hesitated and the lady took over. There was a minute's conversation enlivened with dramatic gestures by the stall holder, clearly expressing horror, insult, grief and then acceptance, after which the scarf was Cathy's for a lot less than the original price demanded.

'Thank you,' she said to Mrs Redcar. 'I would never have dared to offer him so little.'

The lady shrugged, the light of battle fading in her eyes.

'It's a tradition, a way of life. Both the seller and the customer enjoy it. You'll soon get the hang of it, and don't worry if you still feel you paid more than you should. A few pence means a lot more to them than it does to you. It helped that I can speak some basic Egyptian. Is there anything else you are interested in?'

'Not at the moment. Are there any antique shops where you can buy really old things?'

Mrs Redcar gave her a shocked look.

'Egyptians are tired of seeing their works of art taken away to other countries. There are strict laws against taking antiquities out of the country. Of course, there are always people trying to smuggle stuff out because some collectors will pay a fortune for genuine antiquities, but I wouldn't try it.' She looked around. 'I thought Mr Sanderson might have been here to protect you from the traders.'

Cathy scanned the people around them.

'That's odd. He was on the coach coming here, but I can't remember seeing him in the temple.'

'Doubtless he will reappear. Meanwhile, on to the next sight.'

Cathy was grateful for the lunch back

on the boat and the afternoon rest before the excursion in the cool of the evening.

While Cathy spent her spare time in her cabin conscientiously making notes for John Hunter, trying to remember everything that Mavis had said and also reading her guidebook, others had been busy socialising and when she went in to dinner she found that there were changes in the seating arrangements. Another party of Hunter's Tours clients had joined the cruise late the previous night after their plane from another airport had been delayed.

The two groups had soon made contact in the bar and around the swimming pool and now, ignoring the waiters' attempts to seat them at the allotted tables, newfound friends and acquaintances insisted on eating together. The couple who had visited Egypt five times had moved to another table and been replaced by a taciturn young man who introduced himself as Michael Anders and then ate steadily and resisted all attempts to make conversation. Cathy, however, was still seated between Mrs Redcar and Tom Sanderson.

'What happened to you today?' she asked Tom. 'I saw you at the High Dam this afternoon, but you seemed to vanish this morning.'

'A business meeting, I'm afraid. I was sorry to miss the temple at Philae. Tell me about it.'

So she did, once again not noticing how he had avoided having to say anything more about his own activities.

He did not go to the lounge after dinner but Cathy told herself that it was her duty to see how her firm's clients enjoyed their evenings and stayed there after she had finished her coffee. The lounge was full and she found the young man who had sat silently throughout the meal asking if he might take the empty seat beside her. Although he had not made a very favourable impression she could not refuse without seeming impolite, and he put a coffee and a whisky down on the

27

table. She had the impression that it was not the first whisky of the evening.

'Don't worry,' he said as he saw he eyeing the drink. 'I'm not going to get noisy or make advances to you.'

Cathy's jaw set.

'I'm not worried,' she said crisply. 'I assure you I can deal with any trouble.'

He laughed, surprised into spontaneity, and lifted his glass in a mock salute. 'This is to help me sleep. I heard your friend call you Cathy,' he said looking round. 'Your companion, Tom, he isn't here?'

'He's not my companion, I'm here for the cruise on my own. I gather you are too?'

'Yes. I've been working hard, travelling all over Europe. My doctor told me I was suffering from stress and should take a holiday.'

Finally he drained the last of his whisky and left.

'A strange young man,' said Mrs Redcar, sliding into the empty seat. 'I'm not sure about him. Anyway, now you have two young men to talk to as well as an old woman.'

Cathy tried to be tactful, but Mrs Redcar waved her away.

'Don't worry. I'm an old woman and one of my hobbies is observing fellow travellers, and I find both Mr Anders and Mr Sanderson very intriguing. But please be careful.'

'Mrs Redcar, I am twenty-three, I've met a lot of men and had several boyfriends. I don't need to be told to be careful.'

She had expected the other woman to take offence, but instead Mrs Redcar smiled at her.

'Excellent. You have spirit and I think you have brains. However, I have several decades more experience than you, so if you need advice or help please come to me. Meanwhile,' and she waved her glass at an animated group at a nearby table, 'do you see that man over there with Mavis and three other women? I'm sure I've seen him somewhere else and I'm trying to remember where.' She frowned.

The man in question was probably in his sixties, as were the women laughing at his jokes. He was very neatly dressed and groomed, though his blazer looked a little old-fashioned. As Cathy and Mrs Redcar watched, the waiter brought another round of drinks. The man was obviously about to tell the waiter to add them to his bill, but one of the women laid a hand on his arm and spoke to the waiter, who smiled, made a note on his pad and moved away.

There was an exclamation from Mrs Redcar, who was now sitting bolt upright.

'I remember now!'

'Who is he?'

Mrs Redcar glanced at Cathy impatiently.

'I'll have to check with the guide to be sure, but I think I'm right. If so, he's a minor menace if you don't know how to deal with him.'

'In what way?'

'Let me make sure I've identified him correctly first.'

She would not say any more, and soon Cathy decided it was time for bed though she stayed awake for some time mentally reliving the day's experiences and also fretting about the man in the blazer and why he was a potential menace.

Passengers who had decided to take the excursion to the great temple of Abu Simbel left in the early hours. The rest, including Cathy, slept on happily and enjoyed a quiet morning exploring Aswan or relaxing by the pool. Cathy chose this peaceful option. She took her guidebook on deck to read, but it was very restful on the sunbed and soon her eyes closed. When she woke up Tom Sanderson was sitting beside her. Unaware of her regard, he was sitting apparently at his ease, but the shoulder muscles under the thin shirt were tense. He was watching the passengers as they chatted, sunbathed and played in the splash pool, his dark eyes warily considering all of them.

'No business meeting today?' Cathy asked.

He jumped, and then looked down at her in smiling protest.

'Sleeping Beauty should give some warning when she wakes up!'

She ignored the apparent flippancy.

'Is everything all right? You were looking rather grim.'

He laughed dismissively. 'I'm a businessman. For me, everything is all right only when the contract is signed and the cheque is in the bank. How about you? Is the holiday going as you expected?'

She held up the guidebook. 'I'll be happier when I've mastered a few more gods and pharaohs.'

'Didn't you know anything before you booked the holiday? After all, surely you didn't spend your scratch card winnings on a trip to somewhere you knew nothing about.'

This needed more rapid thought. 'I just went in the travel agent's and asked what five-star holidays they had in the next few days. They told about this one and it sounded exciting — a cruise as well as a hotel.'

The long lashes were lowered, veiling his eyes, and she could not tell what he thought of her reply.

'What type of scratch card was it?' he asked.

'Does it matter?'

'I just thought I might buy one when we get back and see if I can get lucky too. Did you spend all your winnings on this holiday?'

This was getting beyond idle curiosity and anyway Cathy was guiltily aware that she needed to work out all the details of her scratch card story. She swung her legs off the sun lounger.

'I think I'll go to my cabin for a bit. I've had enough sun.'

His hand was on her wrist, gently detaining her.

'Before you go, I saw you talking to Anders last night. Did he say anything interesting?'

She stood up, shaking off his grip.

'You ask far too many questions, so I've got one for you. Why do you want to know?'

There was no reply as she hastily gathered up her possessions. When she reached the stairs that would take her below deck she looked back. He was gazing straight ahead again and his expression was unreadable.

Cathy wished she could remember details about him from his booking form, but single travellers were not uncommon in Egypt and there had been no reason to take particular note of him or of Michael Anders.

The tables were half-empty at lunchtime and Cathy was relived that neither Tom Sanderson nor Michael Anders appeared.

It was mid-afternoon when the Abu Simbel excursionists returned, tired but very pleased with their trip and eager to tell all those who hadn't gone how much they had missed. With them safely aboard, the boat set off down the river for its next destination and both Tom Sanderson and Michael Anders appeared for dinner, the former talking politely to anyone who addressed him and the latter again hardly saying a word. Mavis had moved to another table and was sitting next to the man Mrs Redcar had noticed. She saw Cathy looking at the pair and nudged her.

'I'll tell you all about him after dinner,' she murmured conspiratorially.

Later, sitting in the lounge with a large gin and tonic while Cathy nursed a glass of wine, Mrs Redcar began.

'Look round here,' she instructed Cathy. 'What do you notice about the passengers?'

Cathy hoped she could be tactful.

'Well — the majority are quite mature.'

'You mean most of us are pensioners. Go on.'

'There are more women than men.'

Mrs Redcar nodded vigorously.

'Exactly. You've got lots of women, very few men and practically all the men that are here are with their wives.'

'You've got Mr Sanderson, Mr Anders and that man Mavis is talking to.'

'You've got Mr Sanderson and Mr Anders, if you want them. They are not interested in elderly ladies. That leaves Edward O'Neill, or Major Edward O'Neill, as he calls himself.'

'Is he a danger? Should people be warned against him?'

Mrs Redcar shook her head. 'I was wrong to say he was a menace. There are men who make a living by taking advantage of lonely women, but I've decided that Major O'Neill isn't one of them.' She paused to enjoy her drink. 'He is retired, obviously, and I should think he is telling the truth when he says he was in the Army. My theory is that he lives alone and has enough money to manage but very little to spare. However, he wants to enjoy the good life, so he checks on travel firm advertisements and when there is a cheap offer which he can afford, probably a last-minute offer, he takes it.

'It would have to be for a four or five-star holiday, he wouldn't want anything less. Then he can spend a week or more being charming to lonely ladies. The only thing is — he's always a little slow at paying for drinks or taxi rides, or he claims he has left his wallet on the boat or in the hotel, but the ladies are always ready to pay to save him embarrassment.'

'You mean he is taking advantage of them?' Cathy said, shocked at such behaviour in the older generation, but Mrs Redcar laughed.

'Don't be naïve, Cathy. He keeps the ladies amused, and they repay him with drinks, etc. You'll find that most of them know perfectly well what he is doing but think his company is worth the money. The only risk is when one of them doesn't know the rules of the game and gets too fond of him. The disillusionment can be painful.'

'But elderly ladies . . .'

'Elderly ladies, old ladies, have by definition lived a long time. They have had a lot of experience.'

'But you were worried about him yesterday.'

'Then I did some homework. Look at his clothes, Cathy. Very respectable and carefully looked after, but old. A real con merchant would be wearing new, expensive stuff. Major O'Neill just wants a good holiday and good company to make up for the rest of his rather boring life. After all, he is probably lonely most of the time.'

'Why are you telling me?' Cathy asked and Mrs Redcar smiled a little patronisingly.

'Because your little story about the scratch card was not very convincing. Because whenever somebody, like Mavis Elton, criticises something to do with the holiday you look very worried, as if you were personally responsible. You're not a tourist; you are from the travel company. Don't worry, I won't tell anybody. But I warn you, if I have a complaint I will come straight to you.'

Cathy had no reply, and Mrs Redcar left soon afterwards leaving Cathy to brood on what she had been told, until she was distracted when Tom Sanderson sat down beside her.

'I'm not asking you if I can sit here because you might say no,' he told her. 'I'm here to apologise. I was being too inquisitive this afternoon.'

'Far too inquisitive,' Cathy said firmly. 'Now, if you will excuse me . . . '

'When you have finished your drink? And I've just ordered you another one!'

A smiling waiter placed another glass of wine in front of her. She hesitated, torn between her desire to tell Tom Sanderson to go away and her innate politeness, which required her to thank him for the drink. Before she could decide, he hurried on.

'I was asking all those questions partly because I'm naturally inquisitive, and I do find Anders rather puzzling.' He paused, and looked at her from under those long eyelashes. 'And partly because you are the most attractive woman on the boat, and I saw you first.'

Cathy almost choked on her wine. 'You mean I am the only woman under fifty on this boat! Sitting beside me at dinner does not give you any claim on me!'

'I held your hand on the plane when you were terrified of flying.'

'Nevertheless . . . '

She stopped. His eyes were anxiously apologetic, but there was a suspicion of a grin lurking round the corners of his mouth.

'Mr Sanderson, I accept your apology and your wine. Goodnight.'

With that she stood, picked up her glass and made for the door. Behind her, she could hear his laughter.

3

Back in her cabin, Cathy remembered her duty as a daughter and sent her mother a text informing her that not only had she arrived safely but that she was having a wonderful time. She was sure her mother would have loved sitting on deck watching the banks slide by, seeing the egrets in the reeds and the fishermen standing in the river with their nets, and wondered whether she could persuade her parents to try a holiday abroad sometime.

The next morning when she looked out of her window she saw the temple of Kom Ombo looming over the boat. After breakfast it took less than a minute to climb the steps into its precincts.

'Of course, it's very pleasant but it's really quite modern,' said the man who was on his fifth cruise.

'Modern?' Cathy enquired, looking at the engraved walls.

'Graeco-Roman,' he said dismissively. 'Barely two thousand years old, like most of the temples we see along the river. Wait till we get to Luxor. That's the bit I like best.'

'But I find Kom Ombo very attractive,' Michaels Anders interjected.

She had noticed that he had been keeping near her since they left the boat, but this was the first time he had spoken. She smiled at him as they walked on.

'Fancy thinking of something two thousand years ago as fairly modern! I'm still mastering the basics of Egyptian history and gods,' she said ruefully.

'Perhaps in Luxor it will be clearer,' he assured her. He looked tired and drawn. Frowning, he embarked on a rather stilted statement. 'Miss Singleton, I hope you did not get the wrong idea about me the other evening. I do not usually rely on whisky to get me to sleep. The sudden transition from a very busy life in Europe to cruising down the Nile upset me a little, I think.'

Embarrassed, she shrugged her shoulders. 'You were very polite.' There was a pause. 'Are you sleeping better now?'

He nodded. 'Oh, yes. Everything is going well.'

He said the words dutifully but he still had an air of tension, and when she looked at him she noticed the beads of sweat on his forehead. A little uneasy, she began to move away from him but he seized her arm, looking very agitated.

'Please! Stay with me. I need to be with someone.'

She could not refuse his plea, and let him stay near her for the rest of the visit, dutifully pointing out anything which she found interesting but only receiving very brief replies, and she was relieved when it was time to return to the boat and he left her at the gangplank with a muffled, 'thank you'.

The excursion had not gone as she

had planned. She had decided to make it quite clear to Tom Sanderson by her attitude that she did not want his company that morning, before eventually forgiving him, and she felt a little aggrieved that in fact he had not been there to be shown how kind she could be.

Meanwhile the stallholders at the site were having a busy time. This was to be the last full day on the boat, and to mark the occasion there was to be a party on deck that night. Magid, the guide, had told them all that they were expected to appear in Egyptian dress. So anxious tourists were seeking suitable costumes.

'It's just another way of getting money out of us!' Mavis had sniffed. 'I've a good mind not to bother.'

'I, for one, am looking forward to it,' Mrs Redcar announced. 'Some of these costumes are very becoming. Still, if you want to look out of place at dinner it is up to you.'

Mavis hesitated. 'I didn't say I

wouldn't come in costume,' she said at last. 'I'll think about it.'

Cathy did catch a glimpse of Tom Sanderson late in the afternoon. He was boarding the ship carrying a large briefcase. So he had apparently been to yet another mysterious business meeting.

Cathy had found herself a heavily embroidered flowing silky robe in olive green. She had haggled as hard as she could, but the stallholder's smile as he wrapped the garment and handed it to her suggested that he felt he had had the better of the bargain. However, she was very pleased with her reflection in the mirror that evening when she had put the robe on and carefully applied her make-up.

She glanced at her watch. As usual, she was ready too early. When she looked out her window she saw the setting sun making the river water glow, and snatched up her camera. She would fill in the time by going up on deck and taking some photographs.

When she reached the deck waiters were busy everywhere, laying out tables and creating impressive displays of fruit, but she carefully edged her way along the rail to a spot where there was a good view of the river and the setting sun and took half a dozen pictures.

'It is a beautiful evening. I am sure your photographs will be very good.'

She jumped, and turned to see Ahmed, the head waiter, beaming at her.

'We are making sure you have a good party,' he said proudly, waving an arm towards the tables.

It deserved praise, and she congratulated him sincerely before turning back to her photography. Focussing on the road just above the shore, she saw two dark figures come down the steps towards the boat, and when they came within range of the light from the boat she realised that it was Tom Sanderson and Michael Anders. She wondered what such a different pair were doing together.

Just before they reached the boat, the two men turned to face each other, and it was clear from their body language that a violent argument was going on. At one point it even looked as if the pair would come to blows, but Tom Sanderson broke away and strode towards the boat. Michael Anders followed him.

Disturbed by the little scene, Cathy distracted herself by taking photographs of the display on the deck. As she raised her camera for a final shot, Cathy saw Michael Anders come up on deck and she waved at him.

'Look this way, please!'

He turned his head and she pressed the camera button.

'Thank you! That will make a good picture.'

But he was striding urgently towards her.

'Please! I do not like to be photographed.'

She tried to make light of the situation, surprised by his obvious anger. 'It's just a quick snap, something to remind me of you.'

He held out his hand demandingly. This was getting beyond a joke. Suddenly his hand was gripping her camera tightly. 'Let me see!'

She tried to pull her arm away, but his grip grew tighter. 'Give me the camera!'

'Is there any trouble?'

It was the head waiter, aware that something was wrong. Cathy gave a sigh of relief, and at that instant Anders seized the camera from her.

'Give that back!'

The head waiter was beckoning to other waiters who had noticed the little scene.

'Do you need help, madam?'

'The lady does not need help. Everything is all right,' snarled Anders, thrusting the camera back into Cathy's hand. He strode away, shouldering aside the waiters, and disappearing below decks.

'Are you all right, madam?' the head waiter asked her anxiously as Cathy stood massaging her wrist. She managed a smile.

'Yes. I am now. Thank you for your help.'

She made her way back to her cabin, feeling a little shaken by the scene. Then she checked the digital camera, and found to her incredulous fury that Anders had deleted all the pictures on the memory card. Not only the picture of him but also all her photographs of the holiday had been erased!

What a stupid man, and what a fuss to make about a photograph! He must have had his photograph taken for his passport among other official documents, she fumed, so why make such a fuss over a holiday snap? Next time she saw him, she would tell him what she thought of him.

Cathy was not in a good mood as she made her way towards the restaurant for the gala dinner but she was soon caught up in a whirl of passengers enjoying their exotic costumes and paying each other extravagant compliments, and she began to feel better.

A photographer was waiting by the restaurant door, busily insisting that everybody should pose for his camera before they went in to dinner.

'Ha! At least Mr Anders will have to go hungry if he doesn't want to be photographed,' Cathy thought unkindly, before posing for her picture. Then she saw Mrs Redcar and Mavis approaching. Mrs Redcar had settled for a simple dark red robe, heavily embroidered round the high neckline, but Mavis, rather unwisely, was wearing a belly dancer's outfit with a lot of gold decorating a tight bodice over a bare midriff. From Mavis's rather defiant expression, Cathy guessed that the older woman had realised rather too late that the costume did not suit her.

As the photographer lifted his camera someone among the onlookers laughed, an unkind, mocking laugh, and Cathy saw Mavis flinch. Instinctively she took a step forward.

'What a beautiful costume!' she said enthusiastically. 'I love the headscarf with all those little gold coins!'

Mavis perked up and smiled. 'I thought it was very pretty,' she said, smoothing the gauzy skirt.

'As pretty as its wearer,' said a new voice. Major O'Neill, resplendent in a black robe and a white turban, advanced towards Mavis and bowed, straightening to hold out his arm. 'Will you do me the honour of permitting me to take you in to dinner?'

Coyly Mavis took his arm and the couple marched proudly into the restaurant.

'Well done!' Mrs Redcar's voice said quietly next to Cathy. 'You were very kind, and I think the Major has earned himself a brandy tonight.'

Cathy had not been looking forward to the evening — after all, she was now on bad terms with both her possible partners, but to her surprise she found herself enjoying the party. Michael Anders did not appear, and neither did Tom Sanderson. There was a good atmosphere. The tourists were determined to enjoy their last night on board and the crew were determined to send them away happy.

After dinner, everybody took their seats in the lounge for the entertainment, ranging from a whirling dervish to a belly dancer who was athletic rather than erotic. Mrs Redcar was applauding this act politely when she looked at someone behind Cathy, widened her eyes, and gave a very appreciative, 'Ooh!'

It was Tom Sanderson, and no matter what grievance Cathy held against him, she had to admit that he looked magnificent. His suntan was emphasised by a white turban and a white robe bound with a scarlet sash, and his smile had a piratical jauntiness as he swept an impressive bow.

'May I join you?'

Before Cathy could decide whether she was speaking to him or not, Mrs Redcar had made room for him on the couch between her and Cathy.

'You look like the hero out of a film!' Mavis complimented him as she passed by, and giggled when he kissed her hand.

'I'm just glad I was able to get here for part of the evening,' he announced. He smiled at Cathy. She struggled to look cold and aloof and then succumbed to the mood and smiled back. It was clearly assumed by the older tourist that Tom and Cathy were partners, at least for the evening, and when the formal entertainment was over she found herself dancing with him on the small dance floor.

'Am I forgiven?' he said softly.

'For the moment,' she conceded, and saw him glancing around.

'I take it Anders hasn't been seen this evening,' he commented, and then frowned down at her as she made an awkward movement. 'What's the matter? What has he done?'

'Nothing!' she snapped back.

'If he has upset you, I want to know why!'

'I can look after myself, thank you!'

They finished the dance in silence. Tom's smile had vanished and he looked very grim as he led the way back to the couch. Impulsively Cathy took his hand.

'I'm sorry. Mr Anders did something stupid but it wasn't important. Can't we forget him?'

The smile returned instantly. 'Let's go on dancing.'

Much later, the music finally stopped. Looking round, Cathy saw there were very few passengers remaining in the lounge.

'I have enjoyed the evening, and I didn't expect to,' she said. 'And I'll miss the boat when we leave tomorrow. These few days on the Nile have been wonderful.'

'Come and say goodbye to the river,' Tom said, and led her up on deck. Most of the lights had been turned off and they leaned on the rail, watching the moonlight play on the flowing river. It was cool after the heat of the dance floor and Cathy shivered. Tom put his arm around her shoulders and it seemed natural to turn towards him and lift her face to his.

It was a slow, exploratory kiss, and then she released herself gently.

'Tomorrow is going to be a full day. I think it's time I got some sleep,' she said shakily.

Tom did not try to take her in his arms again. 'Goodnight, Cathy,' he said softly. 'I'll see you in Luxor.'

As Cathy got ready for bed she began to feel slightly uneasy. She was always very neat, with everything in its proper place, and she was starting to notice small discrepancies. Her guidebook was under a paperback she was reading, when it should have been on top. The T-shirts in a drawer had the colours mixed and no longer had all the white ones together as she had left them. The zip on her bag of toiletries was undone. At first she wondered if the steward had been prying into her possessions, an idea which made her shudder with distaste.

Anxiously she opened the small personal safe each cabin had hidden in the wardrobe, checked the contents, and gave a heartfelt sigh of relief when she found that nothing was missing. But yet again she was sure that someone had been examining the papers in the safe. She was convinced that her passport and travel tickets had been moved and her notebook where she had been recording details about the holiday was no longer in alignment with the other documents. But none of the money or documents she had put in the safe had been taken.

Cathy sank down on her bed. Her first impulse was to tell the travel rep, Magid, or the captain, that someone had been in her cabin examining her personal items, but she soon realised that she had no concrete proof to offer to anyone in authority. If she told them that a book was out of place, they would be polite, but unconvinced that she was right. Nothing had been taken or damaged, they would point out, so what could she complain about? Yet Cathy knew that someone had been in her cabin and examined everything, even gaining access to the safe.

There had been something very odd about Michael Anders' behaviour, even before the scene over the photograph. Tom had arrived late at the party; so he could have been in her cabin, and Michael Anders had not appeared at the party at all.

She climbed into bed and huddled down under the sheets, glad for the first time that she would be leaving the boat the next day, and slept uneasily until the dawn light marked the start of another morning.

When she woke up, her first thought was the question that she should have asked herself the previous night.

Why had someone gone through her possessions if they did not intend to rob her?

4

Cathy was not the only one feeling rather listless and reluctant to get up the next morning. Enthusiasm for the last excursion from the boat was obviously lacking at breakfast time, and there were several empty seats.

'I can't enjoy a party at night and then get up early to listen to a lecture on Egyptian temple architecture,' groaned one disconsolate traveller.

But Magid bustled around, promising them wonders at the temple, and finally got his little party off the boat in reasonable spirits. Tom came up to her, smiling, obviously expecting a warm welcome after the previous night, but she was still wondering whether he was the person who had searched her cabin and he was clearly taken aback when she gave him a brief, neutral greeting, hurried away from him, and spent the rest of the time close to Mrs Redcar. When she sneaked a look at him later he was frowning blackly.

Cathy looked and listened dutifully when they reached the temple, but sharp eyes could tell that she was not really paying proper attention, and when they returned to the boat Mrs Redcar invited her to have coffee on deck with her. As Cathy sank down gratefully she heard the throb of engines as the boat set off for the last stop, Luxor. Mrs Redcar waited till she had finished her coffee and then leaned forward.

'So what's the matter?'

Cathy jumped. 'Nothing! Why?'

'Because you are looking so miserable. In fact you are looking downright unhappy, so tell me what is worrying you? Is it Tom Sanderson? You were getting on very well with him last night but you were clearly avoiding him this morning. Did he upset you? A little too eager?'

'No! At least, I don't know if it was him.'

Cathy's voice trailed away and Mrs Redcar sat waiting, till finally the girl surrendered.

'I want to tell someone about it, I suppose.' She began her tale.

'So you see,' she finished, 'I can't complain that anything has been damaged or taken. In fact I can't prove that anybody did go through my things last night. But I am absolutely sure somebody did.'

She looked pleadingly at Mrs Redcar. 'Does it sound a stupid story to you?'

Mrs Redcar shook her head. 'You are sure that things were moved. That's good enough for me.' She frowned. 'But I think you are wrong in supposing that it must have been either Mr Sanderson or Mr Anders.'

'Who else could it be?'

'Cathy, Egypt is an important player in Middle East politics and its government does not want anything to interfere with tourism, which is vital to the Egyptian economy. To make sure there are no unpleasant incidents it has to watch out for possible trouble-makers. You must have noticed the armed guards at the temples.'

'I am quite sure that one of the crew, possibly one of the stewards, is really a government agent on the boat to keep a watchful eye on the passengers and the rest of the crew. I didn't believe your cover story about the scratch card. Someone else may have felt the same but suspected that you had more sinister motives than checking matters for a holiday company.'

Cathy held out an agitated hand to stop her.

'Just a minute! Do you mean that somebody might actually have suspected me of being a spy or a troublemaker?'

'Possibly. Possibly they just wanted to check exactly what you were. They may have done the same to other people who didn't notice.'

Cathy shook her head to clear it. 'So you really think it might have been somebody working for the Egyptian security services who went through my room?'

'It's possible. As you say, it certainly wasn't an ordinary thief.' Mrs Redcar snuggled down in her padded seat. 'Anyway, they'll know you are harmless now, so you shouldn't have anything to worry about. Just be glad someone is taking the trouble to check. And, incidentally, neither of the two young men looks capable of picking the lock of a safe. Now, wake me up when it's time for lunch.'

Lunch had an air of anticlimax after the previous night's party. It was the last meal the holidaymakers would eat on the boat and, like Cathy, most of them were torn between regret at leaving the cruise and anticipation of what they would find at Luxor. Tom Sanderson had apparently accepted that Cathy did not want his company because he sat at another table.

Some of the passengers had already packed and then had nothing to do after lunch but sit waiting for the boat to reach the end of its voyage. Cathy packed swiftly and efficiently after the meal, put her suitcase outside the cabin door, and slung her handbag with her documents and money over her shoulder.

When Luxor came into sight it seemed a large, bustling town after the small villages they had seen along the banks of the Nile. The travellers lining the rail as the ship docked eyed the shore appreciatively. Proper shops and large restaurants, imposing hotels and civic buildings awaited them. Luxor would be fun!

Coaches were already lined up ready to take them to various hotels. Hunter's Tours clients were going to a hotel on the banks of the Nile. Major O'Neill, under the cynical eye of Mrs Redcar, was pointing out to Mavis that this would be very convenient.

Magid had told the passengers that they could stay in their cabins until a general announcement called them to Reception to disembark, but the summons seemed a long time coming. Gradually, losing patience, many of them drifted down to Reception where there was a growing buzz of annoyed chatter. They had reached Luxor, transport was waiting, now they wanted to go to their hotels. Magid appeared and was instantly confronted by Mrs Redcar who demanded to know the reason for the delay.

'A minor matter, dear lady. I am sure you will be leaving soon,' he said soothingly, making for the manager's office.

There was a loud crackle. Everyone fell silent. At last an announcement was going to be made! But it was not what they had expected.

'*Will Mr Anders please come to Reception immediately?*'

There was a pause, then a fresh outburst of conversation.

'That young man? He wasn't at lunch, and I don't remember seeing him at breakfast either,' Mavis commented.

'I think he must have been ill. He's missed quite a few meals,' said Major O'Neill.

'I thought he got his nourishment in

the bar,' Mavis said meaningfully.

The call for Michael Anders was repeated twice more, but he did not appear.

Everybody was getting hot and tempers were fraying. Finally the announcement they were all waiting for was made and they poured out of the boat and on to the coaches. Magid got the coach containing Cathy and Mrs Redcar and the rest of the Hunter's Tours' clients.

'Now can you tell us what on earth caused that awful delay?' Mrs Redcar greeted him. The guide looked flustered.

'An administrative matter. Nothing to worry about.'

'And Mr Anders? Where is he?'

Magid shrugged and sat down near the driver. Obviously he was not willing to give them any more information. Cathy noticed that Tom Sanderson was sitting silently at the back, apparently uninterested in the whereabouts of Michael Anders.

The boat had been impressive, but its scope for decoration had been limited to a degree by the fact that it had to function as a river vessel. The Hotel Gregory had no such limitations. Its impressive facade soared upwards for several stories, dwarfing the arriving guests who made their way through the large plate-glass doors and found themselves in an interior which ran riot with marble and gilding lit by immense chandeliers. Even the lifts were lined in marble topped by golden palm leaves.

The rooms were equally palatial, dwarfing the boat's cabins. From the window Cathy could gaze out over grounds which swept down to the river and she could see over the Nile itself to the green ribbon of the farther bank and the sandy desert beyond.

The dining-room was equally impressive and the food excellent, but Cathy's enjoyment was spoiled by a niggling unease. Something was wrong. Michael Anders and Tom Sanderson were both here with Hunter's Tours. Now Anders had vanished, and she could not forget that scene the previous night when the two men had clearly been threatening each other.

After dinner she wandered out into the grounds and down to the Nile bank. It was very quiet and she enjoyed being by herself for once, away from the group, so she jumped when she heard Tom Sanderson's voice behind her.

'It's still beautiful, isn't it, even when seen from the land?'

He moved forward to stand beside her. 'Yes,' she said finally. 'It is still beautiful.'

There seemed nothing more to say, and after a while she began to move away.

'Wait!' Tom said urgently. 'I followed you out here to find out what was wrong. Why have you suddenly decided you don't want anything to do with me?'

She couldn't challenge him about her vague suspicions, but she had to say something.

'I suppose it's because I remembered all the warnings about holiday romances and decided I didn't want to get involved,' she said lightly.

'Involved? One kiss?' he exclaimed, his voice high with disbelief. 'Oh, and I told you that you were attractive. That's not exactly unbridled passion!'

She was glad that he could not see her blush in the darkness. 'I know, it's just that I did have an unfortunate experience in the past, and I didn't want to repeat it.' She was impressed by her growing powers of improvisation.

Tom gave a gusty laugh. 'All right. No more kisses, no more compliments, but surely we can talk to each other? After all, we are now the only two under sixty in the party. I don't want to talk to grannies all the time.'

She found herself laughing reluctantly. 'All right, I suppose I was being a bit oversensitive. So, what do you want to talk about?'

'Luxor? It looks like a good place to have fun, as well as being full of temples. Did you see all the bars and restaurants along the riverbank?'

A few minutes later she found she had agreed to a walk in town. A hundred yards from the Hotel Gregory they were strolling along a wide promenade where elegant women in designer clothes mixed with others dressed in the long traditional Egyptian robes. People tried to persuade the pair to come into their bar or enjoy the delights of their restaurant, but it was all good-humoured and their refusals were met with a shrug, a smile, and a 'perhaps tomorrow'. Finally they allowed themselves to be enticed down some steps into a small establishment over-looking the river where they were offered half a dozen different teas but settled on coffee.

'Hibiscus tea?' Cathy queried, look-ing at the list of available drinks. 'I've never heard of that before.'

'It's very refreshing actually. You get it hot in tiny glasses.'

'I suppose you've had it at your

business meetings?'

There was a very brief pause. 'Yes. I've also had apple tea and lemon tea.'

She leaned back and looked at him steadily. 'Exactly what kind of business are you involved in?'

'Facilitation,' Tom said glibly, but she shook her head.

'Not good enough. Tell me more.'

He drank some coffee, then shrugged. 'Nowadays trade is international, but there can be difficulties about getting finance in the right currency, obtaining import or export licences, arranging transport of goods from one country to another. I facilitate matters where I can.'

She realised that he was apparently giving information while actually telling her very little. She made another valiant attempt.

'What kind of goods?'

'Everything from pots and pans to luxuries.'

'What were the last things you — facilitated?'

He laughed. 'And you said I was too

inquisitive! Actually I'm not going to tell you what I have been dealing with. It would be too embarrassing. I'll just let you speculate.'

She glared at him furiously as he smiled smugly.

'That's not fair!'

'Perhaps not, but I'm not telling you all my business secrets, Cathy Singleton. For all I know, you may be with a rival firm.'

She was silent. Did that mean that while she had been suspecting him, he had been suspecting her? Had he, after all, been the one who had searched her cabin? She gave up.

'Then instead of more information, may I have another cup of coffee?'

When it was time to leave he insisted on paying.

'I'm not ready to become another Major O'Neill.'

'You mean you've realised how Major O'Neill lets everyone else pay for his drinks?' she asked as they started to stroll back.

'Oh, I think everyone has,' he said comfortably. 'If anyone objects, they can avoid him, but I think most of the ladies think his company is worth it and don't begrudge him some little comforts. Anyway, I don't think he will be able to treat himself to any more holidays. I get the impression from one or two things he has said to me that he is finding it increasingly difficult to live on a small income. Have you noticed how much food he manages to get through at each meal? It is almost as if he is a squirrel, storing it up for hard times. He probably has baked beans on toast, not three-course meals, when he is at home.'

They had reached the impressive entrance of the Hotel Gregory and the doorman sprang to admit them.

'I am getting seriously spoiled on this holiday,' Cathy admitted. 'I'm afraid I'll get a taste for it.'

'You'll just have to buy more scratch cards,' Tom said smoothly, only to receive a sharp elbow in the ribs. A receptionist saw the manoeuvre and raised a polite eyebrow. Giggling, they took the lift up and found they were on the same floor. They stopped outside her room.

'Well, goodnight, Miss Singleton,' Tom said with exaggerated politeness and held out his hand. She looked at it with surprise.

'Well,' he said in a voice full of sweet reason, 'if I can't kiss you goodnight, a handshake seems the only option.'

It had been a very pleasant little outing, and she was virtually convinced that Tom Sanderson was an attractive young man who was interested in business, not hiding sinister secrets.

'Idiot!' Cathy said. She put her arms round his neck and drew him down to her. His arms went round her, and this kiss in an impersonal hotel corridor was far more passionate than the embrace under the light of the Egyptian moon had been.

There was a polite cough, and they broke apart quickly. Mrs Redcar and

Mavis were a few feet away. Mrs Redcar's face expressed a certain interest, while Mavis's face showed avid curiosity.

'Er, goodnight, ladies,' Tom managed, and fled in undignified haste. Cathy hurriedly unlocked her door after also bidding the ladies goodnight in a rather shaky voice. Safely inside her room, she shook with laughter. That little episode would provide plenty of gossip for the next day!

Even at breakfast she was aware from certain low-voiced comments and side-long glances that Mavis had been eagerly spreading her story. Cathy held her head high and ate a hearty breakfast (including yoghurt).

'Are you coming to the Valley of the Kings or have you got another business meeting?' Mrs Redcar asked Tom.

'I'm coming to see the Valley,' he said firmly. 'That's one excursion I wouldn't miss for quite a large contract.'

A coach took them along the riverside, across a bridge and through some small villages. Suddenly they were in an alien landscape where no trees or vegetation of any kind could be seen in the sterile hills and valleys of sand. This seemed a very fitting place for the dead. At the end of the Valley of the Kings a hill in the shape of a natural pyramid dominated the skyline.

'This is what I come for,' breathed the tourist who had visited Egypt so many times before.

There were market stalls and an entrance complex to negotiate, and then they were in the valley itself, where only a narrow road and some simple signs indicated that this was where some of the greatest, most powerful and wealthy pharaohs of ancient Egypt had been reverently entombed, though a short introductory lecture reminded the visitors how few burials had escaped the human greed which had led to plundering and destruction in the past and still threatened some sites.

Cathy wondered what was the point of coming if the tombs were empty, but

Tom was eagerly leading her to a doorway behind which lay the dark mouth of a tomb. Inside, a painted corridor sloped down to the burial chamber which held a great stone sarcophagus. Tom was pointing out the roof, painted blue with gold stars, and the little side chambers where the goods of the pharaoh had been stored to accompany him to the afterlife.

Gradually Cathy became aware that all the details of these earthly possessions were subordinate to the great gods of the underworld whose pictures dominated the tomb. Isis, Osiris, Hathor, Anubis — the all-powerful pharaoh would have to await their judgement on his life.

Outside, Tom waited for her verdict. 'Was it worth coming?'

She could only nod, overwhelmed by what she had seen.

They went on to other tombs, and as they walked along the dusty road she noticed the armed guards who stood watching at strategic points. She was aware that there had been at least one tragic terrorist attack in the Valley and was glad to see these protectors stationed everywhere, and she was also reassured when she remembered Mrs Redcar's account of the undercover agents who were trying to prevent any risk to the tourists.

She felt safe, and happy, and when she remembered Michael Anders it was only to feel pleased that he was not here.

5

The excursion had been a revelation
but it had also been hot and dusty and
Cathy decided to have a shower before
lunch. Tom had gone straight from the
coach on some errand into town.
However, as she collected her room key
from Reception, a stranger stepped
forward.

'Miss Singleton? May I have a word
with you?'

He was an Egyptian aged between
forty and fifty, going grey at the temples
and dressed in a rather crumpled
brown suit. Cathy wondered what he
was trying to sell and decided she did
not have time to listen.

'I'm sorry, but I'm tired and I don't
want to buy anything,' she said briefly,
and started to walk towards the lifts,
only to find her way barred by another
stranger. She looked round with a

touch of panic. The reception staff were watching but did not seem inclined to interfere.

'I am afraid I must insist,' said the first man. 'My name is Inspector Hanif, of the Egyptian police. I would like to ask you about Michael Anders.'

'Mr Anders? We met a few times on the boat, that's all.'

'However, we would like to ask you a few questions. If you would come this way, the manager has put a room at our disposal.'

There was unexpected help.

'Then I will come with Miss Singleton.'

It was Mrs Redcar, cool, calm and determined.

'There is no need,' said the inspector and Mrs Redcar's eyebrows rose.

'In my opinion, there is. Miss Singleton is a young girl in a strange country. She needs someone mature to support her.'

Mrs Redcar was obviously not going to go away and Inspector Hanif shrugged impatiently. 'Come if you must, but we are only going to ask a few questions, I assure you.'

The four of them went into a room furnished as an office with a desk, a filing cabinet and some upright chairs. The inspector sat behind the desk, the two women on chairs in front of him and the other man stood silently by the door.

'I'm afraid that Mr Anders seems to have disappeared,' began the inspector. 'He has not been seen since the last evening of your cruise and his bed was not slept in. Naturally, we are trying to find out everything we can that may help us find him. Apparently he talked to you as much as he talked to anyone and something you don't think is important might help us, so we shall be grateful if you will tell us about your meetings with him.'

Cathy told them of the few occasions she had seen Michael Anders, from his first breakfast on board to the last meeting on the boat deck before the party. She gave no details or comments. There was silence after she had finished while the policeman looked at his notes. Then he looked up at Cathy.

'Other passengers have said that Mr Anders seemed to prefer drinking in the bar to eating. Can you comment?'

So they had spoken to Mavis! Giving information to the police must have made her feel really important!

'He did have a glass of whisky one evening when he sat by me,' she said calmly. 'He said it helped him to sleep. I don't know how much he usually drank. And he did miss some meals.'

Once again the inspector made notes in laborious longhand. Mrs Redcar grew impatient.

'Is that all? Can we go now? We need time to freshen up before lunch.'

Inspector Hanif ignored her, his attention still focussed on Cathy. 'You haven't mentioned his quarrel with Mr Sanderson on the last evening, which I understand you witnessed,' he said calmly.

Bother! One of the waiters preparing

for the party must have seen the two men as well, and seen her watching. She flushed.

'I only saw the two of them from a distance and it was almost dark, so I don't know what happened or what they said. You must ask Mr Sanderson about that.'

'I will in due course. Neither have you given details about your encounter with Mr Anders when he came on board afterwards. There was some trouble about a camera, wasn't there?'

A waiter again, possibly the agent Mrs Redcar had suspected was on the boat. Briefly and reluctantly Cathy recounted how Michael Anders had objected to being photographed and had deleted her picture of him.

'You are sure he deleted it?' the inspector pressed her.

'Quite sure. I checked carefully. He deleted all my photographs.'

Showing emotion for the first time, the inspector threw his pen down on the desktop.

'That is a great pity. Mr Anders seems to have taken his passport with him, wherever he is. A photograph of him would have been very useful.'

'If that's all you want, I can probably supply that,' said Mrs Redcar briskly. 'I took some photographs of the passengers as we were going round temples, just as souvenirs. I think I may have one of Mr Anders.'

Inspector Hanif's face lit up.

Mrs Redcar took her camera out of her capacious handbag, pressed some buttons and handed it to the policeman.

'Look. There he is.'

The inspector looked at the viewer on the digital camera and gave an audible sigh of relief. 'May I have this?'

'You may have the memory card but you don't need the camera. Incidentally, I shall be grateful if you will return the card as soon as possible. I don't want to lose my pictures.'

Inspector Hanif stood up, smiling broadly. 'You will have it back later today. I am most grateful. Good day, ladies.'

The silent guard stood aside as they left the room.

'That is the first time I have been interrogated by a policeman,' Cathy said weakly. 'I feel exhausted. I must have a shower now.'

'The shower can wait a few minutes,' Mrs Redcar announced. 'I am going to order us pre-lunch gin and tonic on medicinal grounds.'

Cathy had to admit she appreciated the cold alcohol.

'I wonder what has happened to Michael Anders?' she mused.

'He probably got drunk in some bar and missed the boat sailing because he was sleeping it off,' was Mrs Redcar's opinion.

'But then why did he take his passport?'

'I don't know.' Mrs Redcar was looking thoughtful. 'But I do wonder why an inspector was sent to find out what has happened and why he wanted so much detail.'

Cathy did not see Tom till dinner. Some other guests had been questioned by the police and were speculating about Michael Ander's fate, though most agreed with Mrs Redcar that he had probably been fast asleep in some bar when the boat sailed.

'He'll probably hitch a lift to Luxor on another boat,' somebody guessed.

'Something else might have happened to him. He could have been robbed,' was another offering.

Tom said nothing.

As they left the dining-room, Cathy slipped her arm through is. 'Come to the lounge. I want to talk to you,' she murmured.

'And I want to talk to you, so let's go ashore. We can have more privacy in one of the bars.'

In a few minutes they were seated overlooking the Nile, each with a coffee and a glass of water.

'I want to talk to you about Michael,' Cathy began reluctantly. 'The police know that you and he quarrelled on the night he disappeared. I saw you on the steps, but I wasn't going to tell them. Unfortunately a waiter saw you as well and knew I'd been watching you.'

Tom grimaced. 'I know. I spent an uncomfortable hour with Inspector Hanif this afternoon.'

He stopped, Cathy waited, staring at him impatiently.

'Well?'

He leant back and gave her a crooked smile. 'I told him that we quarrelled over you.'

Cathy nearly dropped her cup. 'You said what?'

'I told him that Michael Anders had apparently decided you were his girl for the holiday, thought I was trying to take you from him and threatened me if I didn't leave you alone.'

'But that's nonsense! I thought the man was very odd. I've seen very little of the two of you and I'm certainly not romantically attracted to either of you.' She stopped abruptly.

Tom was trying to look hurt. 'You mean you're not in love with me? What about that passionate kiss we shared outside your room last night? The one Mavis witnessed! Don't you think she's told the inspector about that, especially if he asked if there was any reason Anders and I should quarrel?'

'Bother Mavis! I hope you told Inspector Hanif that there was no reason for either of you to be jealous of the other.'

'I told him that, but I am not sure that he believed me.'

Cathy was gazing round her with dawning realisation.

'And if we are seen sitting here together, everybody will believe Mavis's stories. Let's get back to the hotel!'

Tom leant forward, his smile genuine now. 'Look, Cathy, Michael Anders obviously had problems. Just be glad he has disappeared. With any luck, when he reappears he will be put on the next plane home before he can cause any more trouble. Meanwhile, we still have a few days in one of the most fascinating places in the world. Let's enjoy each other's company and forget about Michael Anders, Mavis and other gossips.'

There was a pause while Cathy considered what he had said, and then she lifted her cup in a mock toast.

'Why not? Let us enjoy our holiday.'

They spent the evening wandering along the riverfront. At one time they found themselves looking at rows and rows of great floodlit columns.

'Karnak,' Tom had announced, almost with awe. 'One of the greatest temples in the world.'

'You really love these temples and monuments, don't you?' Cathy commented.

'When I was young I was taken to see the exhibition of Tutankhamun's treasures when they were brought to London. It fascinated me and I read everything I could find about Egypt and its history. When I first came to Egypt I went to Cairo and saw the Pyramids, then came to the Valley of the Kings. I felt I had achieved my life's ambition.'

Cathy sighed. 'I know it has a great past, but what about modern Egypt?'

His voice was suddenly very serious. 'Egypt is important — a bridge between extremes. What happens in Egypt nowadays may be as important to the rest of the world as what happened when Antony met Cleopatra all those years ago.' He stopped and gave an embarrassed laugh. 'I care about Egypt. Let us leave it at that.'

Tom was a good companion. It became obvious that he had travelled widely and he had a fund of stories. Cathy found herself laughing aloud, attracting amused glances from passers-by. In return she told him of her holiday experiences in England.

'I can never decide what is best,' he commented, 'whether to get to know one place very thoroughly or to wander the world and try everything.'

'Well, I thought England provided enough variety,' Cathy said thought-fully. 'I think I shall still spend most of my holidays there. It's got beautiful country and thousands of years of history, but I may come abroad sometimes. Of course, I won't have you to hold my hand in the aeroplane.'

'You never know,' Tom said casually. 'Now, do you want a goodnight coffee here or where we went last night?'

It was late when they finally returned to the hotel; Tom's arm companionably round Cathy. They said goodnight to the receptionist, and Cathy recognised a figure standing in the background. It was the man who had accompanied Inspector Hanif. Presumably that meant that Michael Anders had not yet reappeared.

This was made clear the following morning. Mavis had been asking questions.

'Apparently no-one had found any trace of him,' she told Cathy. 'The police showed Mrs Redcar's picture of him to all the bars and cafes and they all said they hadn't seen him.' One hand fidgeted uneasily with her necklace. 'I have felt very safe in Egypt, but this is disturbing.'

Cathy had a sudden flash of insight into how this elderly woman must feel. She had thought herself quite brave, coming alone to this exotic land. Now things didn't seem quite so safe and she was frightened.

'Don't worry,' she said gently. 'After all, young men are always getting themselves into scrapes and they seem to survive. Perhaps he fell in love at first sight and couldn't bear to leave the girl!'

Mavis giggled and began to look a little brighter. 'You may be right, though he didn't look very romantic. Fortunately you and Mr Sanderson don't appear to be having any problems. Staying at the same hotel must be very convenient.'

Magid announced the arrival of their coach before Cathy had time to think of a suitable, polite, response.

Tom had told her that he had to visit a firm in Luxor, so Cathy had no distractions as she listened to Magid's clear exposition of the long and complicated history of the Karnak complex. Afterwards the group was free to wander round the site and concentrate on what impressed them most. Cathy was craning her neck to look up at the enormous columns in the Hypostyle Hall when somebody spoke to her.

'They are very impressive, aren't they?'

It was an Egyptian, a man dressed in a formal dark suit, which did not seem to go with his tough face and broken nose. Cathy smiled, nodded and moved away, but five minutes later she found him beside her again as she studied some carvings.

'These are very old, but very well preserved,' he pointed out.

They had been warned against individuals who might try to attach themselves to them as personal guides and then demand payment, so this time Cathy looked at him coldly.

'I know. Our guide told us that,' she said. This time he seemed to take the hint and did not speak to her again, though she did notice him among the crowds of tourists making their way from one site to another. Perhaps he was looking for an easier victim.

The morning passed quickly and when she looked at her watch she found it was time to return to the coach. She had left the temple and was crossing in front of a car on one of the roads in the car park when she heard her name.

'Miss Singleton!'

It was the man who had spoken to her twice in the temple. Now he was standing by the open door of the car and beckoning her. She turned her head away and started to cross the road, but suddenly her arms were gripped from behind and she was thrust towards the car, where the first man was now in the driving seat with the engine revving loudly. Before she could scream there was a hand across her mouth and she was being pushed towards the open door. Then she heard a shrill scream and an indignant roar.

'What are you doing? Let her go at once!'

Somebody else ran towards the car and the grip on Cathy slackened as her attacker turned to face this challenge. Major O'Neill had come to her rescue! She twisted desperately, ducked under a flailing arm and dived for freedom, only to collide with Mavis, whose screams were now attracting attention all round. Cathy looked back at the car just in time to see Major O'Neill being thrown to the ground by a man who climbed into the car and slammed the door shut as the car roared away.

Cathy, feeling suddenly very weak, found she was now trying to support Mavis, who had abandoned screaming in favour of an apparent fainting fit. Cathy's knees gave way and the two women collapsed in an undignified heap on the tarmac. Meanwhile Major O'Neill had picked himself up and was ruefully examining his blazer. Soon

Magid was hurrying towards them. Waving aside offers of help from the small crowd that had formed, he and other members of the group got the three of them back on the coach, where Cathy managed to explain what had happened.

'I saw him speak to you when you were by the car,' one of the group commented, 'but I'd seen you talking to him in the temple, so I thought you knew him.'

'I've never seen him before,' Cathy said shakily. She turned to Major O'Neill. 'I couldn't have stopped them pushing me into the car. If it hadn't been for you, they would have kidnapped me.'

'But who were they? Why should they want to kidnap you?' somebody else asked.

Inspector Hanif asked the same questions later, and Cathy had no answers.

'Perhaps it was a mistake and they thought I was someone else,' was her rather lame suggestion.

'Perhaps,' he said, obviously thinking very little of the idea.

He sat back and looked at her thoughtfully. 'Miss Singleton, you were the last person to speak to Michael Anders, and now you have been the victim of an apparent kidnapping plot. I have to ask myself if there is any connection.'

Cathy shook her head. 'None as far as I know. I am an ordinary tourist here on holiday.'

'Is that the whole truth? There is this story of some lucky bet.'

Cathy decided it was time to tell him everything and explained how John Hunter had sent her to check on the holiday.

'So you are a kind of industrial spy?' Inspector Hanif said, his brow wrinkling.

'No! I'm just having the same holiday as everyone else, and when I get back I shall tell my employer what was good about it and what could be improved.'

He was twisting his pen uneasily in his fingers. 'I will do my best to find out the truth behind this attack. Meanwhile, you are an intelligent young woman and you will understand if I ask you not to make a fuss. Tourism is important to us.'

'Selling safe holidays is important to us,' retorted Cathy, but then relented. 'I have loved what I have seen of Egypt. I will not do anything to harm its tourist trade.'

6

The incident had upset Cathy. She felt shivery in spite of the warm sun and spent most of the afternoon cuddled up in bed, although she scolded herself for being so foolish and wasting precious hours of her holiday.

As the sun began to set there was a knock on her door, which she had locked. 'Who's there?' she demanded sharply, sitting up in bed.

'Me. Tom Sanderson.'

When she opened the door she saw him standing outside with a tray bearing two cups of coffee and two brandies.

'You don't have to have the brandy,' he told her, 'but I thought it might be good for you.'

She scrambled back into the warmth of her bed, leaning against the pillows as Tom carefully placed the tray on the bedside cabinet, sat on the edge of the bed, and handed her the coffee, which was certainly welcome, spreading warmth and comfort through her body. Tom sat watching her silently and then handed her a glass and she found that a few sips of brandy did indeed help her relax.

'Thank you,' she said with real gratitude. 'I feel such a fool. It was a stupid incident, over in a couple of minutes.'

'Somebody tried to kidnap you. You are entitled to be upset.'

She was dismayed to find her eyes filling with tears. 'But why should anyone want to do such a thing? I'm not rich. They couldn't hold me to ransom!'

'I've heard half a dozen different versions of what happened. Could you tell me what actually took place?'

Prompted by his occasional question, Cathy gave him a detailed account of the morning.

'So one of the men tried to make some contact with you in the temple, and they knew your name,' he said thoughtfully. 'That means it was planned in advance.'

'But why me?'

There was no obvious answer.

'Anyway, you're safe in the hotel,' Tom said bracingly. 'Have a long bath, put on your prettiest dress and get ready for dinner. I bet you didn't eat much lunch.'

'I didn't have lunch! I was talking to Inspector Hanif and then all I wanted to do was curl up here.'

'Then you'll really enjoy your dinner and you will be quite safe with Mrs Redcar on one side and me on the other.'

In fact she was extremely hungry by dinnertime. Mrs Redcar called for her as soon as the gong sounded.

'You see — we won't even let you walk to the dining-room by yourself,' the lady pointed out smugly.

Waiters and guests who had heard about the incident at the temple fussed over her gratifyingly and she was surprised how much she enjoyed her meal.

'Of course,' Mrs Redcar remarked, 'Major O'Neill will be here soon, checking on how you are.'

In fact the Major appeared literally seconds after Cathy walked into the lounge with Tom and Mrs Redcar on either side, and she found herself wondering whether he had been watching for her appearance. Anyway, she was aware of her very real debt of gratitude to him and thanked him warmly. He appeared genuinely pleased and accepted her offer of a whisky.

'I am just glad that I could be of assistance,' he assured her. 'Nowadays I sometimes feel a bit old and useless, so it made me feel good to be able to help you by tackling those ruffians.'

He was wearing a light linen jacket, Cathy noticed.

'How is your blazer?' she asked anxiously.

He shook his head sadly. 'I'm afraid it suffered more than I did. I have looked at it, but mending it is beyond my sewing skills.'

'Bring it round tomorrow morning,' Mrs Redcar intervened. 'Let me have a look at it.'

'Would you? I shall be most grateful for anything you can do, so long as it's not too much trouble. I've had it a long time and I'm rather fond of it.'

'I'll do my best for it. Now, can I buy you another drink?'

Tom had been very quiet over dinner, but now he turned to Cathy.

'Are you coming out tomorrow? It would be a pity to miss the Tombs Of The Nobles. It's very different from the Valley Of The Kings. Several of them are actually in a village and you have to keep diving down holes in the ground between houses.'

'Oh, I'll be ready for that,' Cathy assured him. 'All I need is a good night's sleep.' She looked over at Major O'Neill, now deep in conversation with Mrs Redcar. 'Will you do me a favour? When I've gone, buy the Major some more drinks and I'll pay you for them tomorrow.'

'I'll definitely get him as much whisky as he wants and I'll pay for it,' Tom said firmly.

Soon Cathy announced that she was tired and left after thanking the Major for his bravery yet again. She did feel much better, but still took care to lock the door before she went to bed.

The incident at the temple seemed like a bad dream when she awoke. After breakfast she saw Mrs Redcar and recognised Major O'Neill's precious blazer hanging over her arm.

'Are you really going to mend it?' she asked, and Mrs Redcar shook her head firmly.

'Not me. I've already arranged for one of the hotel staff to take it to be invisibly mended this morning. The Major will be delighted and won't know I haven't slaved over it.'

Cathy was about to offer to pay for the blazer to be mended but Mrs Redcar gave her a steely glare.

'Don't you dare say you'll pay. I've decided the Major has many good points really and I'm going to treat him.'

'Won't Mavis be jealous?' Cathy risked mischievously, but Mrs Redcar lifted her brows in surprise.

'Haven't you heard? Oh no, you did go to bed rather early last night. Mavis has taken umbrage. Apparently she got very annoyed when everyone started praising Major O'Neill for his bravery in rescuing you. She was physically trying to hold him back when he was trying to reach you. She felt he should have stayed with her and made sure she was safe.'

'I thought her faint was a bit sudden.'

'An attempt to reclaim the limelight, I think. Anyway, there are still plenty of other mature ladies willing to pay for the Major's coffees this morning.'

Only a small group had decided that the tombs of Egypt's ancient nobles were worth visiting. Mavis was there, Mrs Redcar, Cathy and Tom and a quartet of friends.

'It is better to have only a few of you,' Magid told them. 'The tombs are small and some are down very narrow steps.'

Once over the Nile, they soon arrived at a village of higgledy-piggledy houses where Magid led them through streets that were sometimes little more than passageways. Then, as he guided them down unexpected stairways, they realised that many of the tombs were actually under the village houses.

The tombs were indeed very different from those of the Pharaohs. Instead of gods, the walls showed family pictures such as a father fishing while his daughter sat beside him. The scenes were charming, and in some ways spoke more directly to the tourists than the royal tombs. Not everybody agreed, of course. Mavis was inclined to sneer at the comparative smallness of the tombs and shrieked in protest at the steep descent she had to make to see some of them.

Temporarily on the surface, Cathy lagged behind the rest of the party when she saw a tempting array of carved plaques and had to hurry after them. Mavis beckoned her imperiously.

'Come on! I don't want to get lost here.'

Cathy looked round but for once there was no-one to be seen. 'Where have they all gone?'

'Over there!' Mavis said impatiently, pointing to a house on the edge of the village. 'They went round the corner.'

Cathy hurried round the corner and found an Arab holding a door open.

'This way, madam,' he instructed her, directing her into the ground floor room and then stepping back to reveal the first steps of a flight going down beneath the ground. Obediently Cathy started to descend, but then hesitated.

'I can't hear anyone,' she said to the Arab as he loomed over her. 'Are you sure my friends are here?'

Before the Arab could reply she heard her name being called urgently and Tom Sanderson burst through the doorway.

'I'm here!' she said, and then hands grasped her round the waist and pulled her roughly down the stairs. She heard a scuffle above her and was abruptly aware of being thrust into a dark chasm before she hit her head on the floor and lapsed into unconsciousness.

She woke up in total darkness, lying on some hard surface. Someone was swearing softly but with great feeling, and in English.

'Tom?' she said hesitantly.

'Stay where you are,' he replied.

There was a shuffling sound, then his fingers touched her and soon she was sitting with his arm supporting her.

'What happened?' was the obvious question, so she asked it.

'I was looking for you and saw you going into some house so I came after you and got hit on the head. What were you doing?'

'I thought it was the next tomb. An Arab was beckoning me and Mavis was pointing at it.'

Tom groaned, and she felt that he

was rubbing his head.

'Yesterday someone tried to kidnap you, so today you wander off on your own and when some stranger asks you into their house you wander straight in! Haven't you any common sense?'

Cathy sat up indignantly, pushing his arm away. 'It looked just like the entrance to some of the other places!'

Before she could think of a biting reply they were both struck dumb by the sound of a groan. Cathy found herself back in Tom's arms.

'There's someone else here!'

'Keep quiet so we can locate them.'

They listened and could just make out the sound of hoarse breathing, but it was difficult to locate the sound. Cathy began to pat the ground around her.

'Tom, see if my bag is here somewhere. There's a torch in it.'

It took a couple of minutes of unnerving exploration by touch of the uneven floor, but finally Cathy felt the soft cotton of her bag. Very carefully she undid the zip and fumbled in it until she could grasp the small torch, which her mother had insisted she should bring. She pressed the button and a narrow beam of light pierced their surroundings.

They were in a rough cellar apparently dug out of the ground and at the bottom of the opposite wall was a mattress with a figure lying on it. When they bent over it, they saw that it was Michael Anders. He was unconscious, with dark blotches on his head and shirt. Cathy's heart gave a thump as she realised that the patches were blood.

'Shine the light on him,' Tom commanded and began to examine Michael Anders gently. Then he sat back on his heels and sighed. 'I can't see any bad wounds, but he's lost quite a lot of blood, he's obviously dehydrated, and his skull may have been damaged.'

Anders groaned again and moved one clenched fist slightly. His eyelids flickered. Cathy was rummaging in her bag again and triumphantly produced a small plastic bottle of water.

'I've got this, and some wet wipes to clean him up a bit.'

Tom held the bottle carefully to Ander's lips and even though the young man's eyes remained closed his throat moved as he swallowed a couple of mouthfuls. Tom gave the bottle back to Cathy and took the wet wipes she held out. She realised how thirsty she was and wiped the neck of the bottle with her handkerchief before taking a drink, only to find Tom's hand taking the bottle from her.

'I want some more!' she said indignantly.

He took a mouthful and then screwed the top back on the bottle.

'So do I,' he said grimly, 'and so does he,' indicating Anders with a nod. 'But this is all the water we have and we don't know how long we'll be here. Give me the torch for a minute.'

He crossed to the door, examined it carefully, tried to get a ginger hold on the edge, and then came back, shaking his head.

'I can't open the door, it's too strong.'

'Then what do we do?'

He sat down on the floor beside her again. 'We wait till somebody comes. Meanwhile, as we don't know how long that will be, you'd better turn off the torch and save the battery.'

They sat together in the darkness, each with their own thoughts, until Cathy stirred.

'Tom? Suppose nobody comes?'

'Someone will come — eventually.'

After an interminable wait, Cathy switched the torch on again. This time she gave Anders a little more water. He moaned and reached out as if he wanted more, but Cathy kept it out of his reach, barely moistening her own lips. She was going to pass the bottle to Tom but he was on his feet, rapping at the walls.

'It's possible that some neighbour's cellar may be next to this one. Perhaps we can make a noise and attract attention.' He paused by one section and rapped again. 'I think this bit is hollow.' He looked down at Cathy and forced a smile. 'I suppose you haven't got a miniature pickaxe in that bag, have you?'

She managed to smile back. 'That is about the only thing my mother didn't make me bring.'

Soon he came and sat by her again, the torch was switched off, and thick darkness swallowed them.

'This was going to be the holiday of a lifetime,' Cathy murmured after a while. 'It was going to be sun, sights and luxury. Now I wish I'd gone walking in the Lake District instead.'

She felt, rather than heard, Tom chuckle. 'I know. I wish I was in some pleasant anonymous office arguing about percentages and discounts for quantity.'

More time elapsed. 'We've missed lunch, of course, and I didn't have much breakfast,' Cathy said sadly.

Half an hour later there was a touch of panic in Cathy's voice. 'It is getting very stuffy. There isn't any way for more air to get in, is there?'

'We don't need to worry about lack of air for a long time. Look, Cathy, if someone had wanted us dead they would have killed us and Anders, not just locked us in.'

'I wonder how he got here.'

'It will be some time before he's in a fit state to tell us.'

Incredibly, Cathy found herself drifting into sleep. Her head grew heavier on Tom's head and she gave a gentle snore.

Suddenly he pushed her off him abruptly and she woke up as she hit the floor. In a few seconds she remembered where they were and what had happened.

'What's the matter now?' she said indignantly.

'Shut up! Listen!'

She obeyed. The silence was unbroken and she was just about to express her annoyance when, from somewhere above them, there was the slightest sound of footsteps overhead.

'Shout! We've got to make them hear us!' Tom commanded.

'Suppose they are the ones who put us here?'

'Don't be stupid! They'll know we are here. Now, scream!'

Tom was shouting, calling for help, but Cathy felt petrified. How could she just open her mouth and scream? Then she found she was doing just that, but only a pathetic bleat emerged. She took a deep breath and tried again and this time a full-throated scream emerged. She screamed again and again, but when Tom told her to stop and listen the footsteps could no longer be heard. Had whoever it was gone away?

'Come back!' she yelled. 'We are down here!'

Now the footsteps were back, moving faster. There were muffled noises, and then at last someone was banging on the door. Cathy had her torch on now and was staring at the door, but it did not give way.

'We are getting help!' shouted a man's voice, Magid's voice, and a short time later there were violent blows on the door, and soon an axe-head had penetrated the planks. A minute later and the door was demolished. Magid was outside, holding a big torch, together with four other men, and behind them Cathy for some reason was not surprised to see Mrs Redcar.

'Are you all right?' was Magid's first question.

'We are,' Tom said hurriedly, 'but Anders needs a doctor urgently.'

'Anders?'

Magid stared and then hurried across the room, saw Ander's face and turned to shout instructions in Arabic.

'We will send for an ambulance,' he told Cathy and Tom. 'Meanwhile, let us get you out of here.'

It took an effort to climb the flight of stairs. At the top Mrs Redcar hugged her in a surprising show of emotion.

'I knew you were still somewhere in the village,' she said fiercely. 'I made them look everywhere. I wouldn't give up.'

'I am so glad you didn't,' said Cathy, and fainted.

7

Inspector Hanif was annoyed. He was upset. In fact, Cathy realised, he was furious. 'Tell me again,' he said with careful control. 'This was the second attempt to kidnap you in two days and you still have no idea why anyone should do this to you.'

Cathy shook her head again. 'Honestly, I don't know why it happened to me. I've never been to Egypt before, and all I've done is behave like any other tourist.'

The inspector turned to Tom. 'You, I can understand. You followed Miss Singleton, saw her being encouraged to go into a house, and you were attacked when you tried to reach her. Can you add anything to that?'

'No,' Tom said flatly. 'you already know that our friend, Mavis, was responsible for sending us to the house.'

Mavis had been shrill in self-defence. 'I told Miss Singleton I thought the group had gone to that house because I did see someone going into it. The young man, Mr Sanderson, went dashing after her. Then Magid came back to find the stragglers, saw me and called me.'

'Why didn't you tell Magid where the other two were?'

'I thought they would have the common sense to come looking for the group when they found it was the wrong house.'

'And when they didn't rejoin the group?'

Mavis had shrugged. 'It seemed obvious that the two of them had decided to go off somewhere else.'

In fact, when Magid had begun to worry about Cathy and Tom's disappearance, most of the group had assumed that the young couple had got tired of inspecting tombs and gone off to find something more amusing. However, when they were still missing when it was time to take the coach back to the hotel, Magid, overruling the protests of the rest of the group, had sent the tourists back in the coach but remained in the village to look for the missing pair.

Mrs Redcar had insisted on staying with him. When they had inspected the obvious places such as the cafés and shops and found nothing, she had demanded that the police be called to carry out a house-to-house search, reminding Magid that he had already lost one tourist, Michael Anders, and did not want to lose two more.

'At least I can make sure that you are safe for the rest of your holiday,' Inspector Hanif announced grimly. 'One of my men will stay close to you all day and be outside your room at night.'

'Thank you. I shall feel much better knowing that,' Cathy said, gathering up her remaining scraps of dignity, and she and Tom were finally allowed to go.

'He needn't worry,' she said passionately once they were outside the door.

'I'm going to stay in the hotel, sunbathe and swim in the pool. That should be safe.' She managed a smile. 'If I hadn't followed Mavis's directions you wouldn't have followed me and got stuck in that cellar. I'm sorry about that.'

'Well, at least we got Anders to hospital in time. Apparently he is in a pretty bad way and the police won't be able to question him for some days.'

That night when she opened her door a crack to check before she went to bed, Hanif's subordinate was sitting outside on a chair. He gave her a half-smile and she shut the door, scampered across the room to the bed, and slept soundly all night.

He was seated at a table near her in the dining-room the next morning when she had breakfast, and when she went out to the pool he followed at a polite distance. She began to wonder when he got any sleep.

Mrs Redcar appeared soon afterwards, carrying a large towel, a book, and suntan lotion. Cathy thanked her again for helping Magid look for her. The older woman shrugged.

'Well, I wasn't coming back to the hotel without you, and I was able to persuade Magid quite easily that the scandal that would erupt if he lost two more clients would outweigh any bad publicity caused by calling in the police.'

She looked round for a waiter so that she could order a coffee, but they were all busy. In contrast, when Cathy lifted a summoning finger five minutes later, three waiters almost fought to be the first to reach her.,

'Everybody is very eager to help me today,' Cathy frowned. 'One waiter was hovering over me all through breakfast, asking if I wanted more coffee, offering to get me more toast.'

'Haven't you guessed why?' asked Mrs Redcar, and Cathy shook her head.

'There have been two attempts to kidnap you, and you keep claiming you don't know why. Now, your story about the lucky scratch-card win was far from convincing. So most of the guests have been speculating wildly and then sharing their guesses, with the result that most of the people in the hotel — staff as well as guests — have decided that you are really a wealthy heiress who could afford to pay a large ransom, and that is what your kidnappers are after.'

Cathy stared at her blankly. 'They think I am rich? Oh, if only that were true!' She sat up, frowning. 'But it's not. How can I convince them of that? What shall I say to them?'

Mrs Redcar smiled coldly. 'You can't say anything. The more protest that you are not a rich heiress, the more they will believe you are. Just enjoy the superb service you are going to get, and don't worry about the reproachful looks you will get at the end when you don't give enormous tips.'

Cathy started to giggle, then to laugh, and ended up crying with laughter. Mrs Redcar regarded her calmly.

'That should do you good,' she commented. 'I expect it has released a lot of tension.'

It had. Cathy felt a lot better and thoroughly enjoyed the attentive service she received at lunch before she retreated for an afternoon siesta, reflecting that it was a much better way of passing the time than the previous day had been.

When she left her room later she was pleased to see that she had a new bodyguard. She had begun to feel quite uneasy about the long boring hours of surveillance which the former man had sat through.

No sooner had she settled by the pool than Mrs Redcar picked her way through the sunbeds and sat down next to her. Cathy raised an eyebrow.

'I'm beginning to suspect that you are watching over me as well as that poor man.'

'Of course,' said the other woman. 'Two guards are better than one. Besides, I enjoy your company. And here comes someone else to look after you.'

It was Tom Sanderson, looking hot and tired. He greeted them, sank down and ordered a long cool drink.

'A hard day's facilitating?' Cathy said smoothly.

'Very hard, very hot, very boring. I think I'll change careers and become a beachcomber in Australia instead.' He shut his eyes and leaned back. 'Just let me rest for ten minutes and then I'll go for a shower and change my clothes.' In fact, after five minutes there was a gentle snore.

'Let him sleep,' said Mrs Redcar sympathetically. 'He's got plenty of time to shower before dinner. Anyway, I think the two of you should stay in the hotel this evening. If you step outside the door you will probably have Luxor's police force shadowing you.'

Cathy shivered in the sunshine. 'I don't want to go out. I'd be looking at everyone, wondering whether they were the people who kidnapped me and whether they would try again.' She looked thoughtfully at Tom. 'You know, until we were locked in together yesterday, I thought he might be involved in some peculiar happenings. He did quarrel with Michael Anders and he keeps vanishing to these vague business meetings.'

Mrs Redcar lowered her voice. 'If you are going to consider all the possibilities, have you thought that perhaps he arranged yesterday's kidnapping and only pretended to be a victim?'

Cathy grappled with this new theory.

'Why on earth should he do that?'

Mrs Redcar shrugged.

'I know it's unlikely, but it might have been a way of diverting suspicion from himself and making sure that Michael Anders was found before it was too late.'

Cathy shook her head. 'That's too complicated. Incidentally, I saw Magid after lunch and asked how Michael Anders was getting on. Apparently he is still unconscious but they feel he is getting better. Magid seemed happier to have a client in hospital than one who had mysteriously disappeared.'

It was a very pleasant day, ending after dinner with an hour spent in the hotel's garden, sitting beside Tom Sanderson under the brilliant stars and gazing across the Nile. As he talked, his love of Egypt and its history was very clear.

'I do want to see more,' Cathy sighed. 'One day in the hotel has been enough. I keep thinking what I'm missing.'

'I could take you to the Luxor Museum tomorrow,' Tom suggested. 'It has some really lovely things which you must see. We could go by taxi and your bodyguard could come with us.'

He turned his head sufficiently to see the shadowy figure of the patient guard sitting some yards behind them.

'I do find his presence rather inhibiting.'

Cathy was pleased at the idea of a visit to the museum, especially as it would be in Tom's company. The more she saw of him, the more she liked him.

There was no goodnight kiss when Tom finally escorted her back into the hotel, however. The lurking figure of the police guard certainly discouraged that.

At ten o'clock the next morning Cathy hurried down the stairs to the reception area. Tom was already waiting.

'The hotel has got a taxi for us,' he greeted her, and then looked past her. 'Where's your shadow?'

She looked around. Her bodyguard was nowhere to be seen. 'He was near me at breakfast,' she said uncertainly, and then smiled. 'There he is!'

The unobtrusive figure in the brown suit which Cathy was beginning to think must be standard issue for the Luxor police force hurried towards them. She frowned.

'This is a different man.'

Tom had a few quick words with the man and reassured her.

'He says he is on the day shift and has just relieved the man who was watching you last night. He is also quite happy to come to the museum.'

'The museum? Are you going to Luxor Museum?'

It was Mavis, sharp-eared and ruthless at getting something she wanted.

'I was going to go there. Can I come with you? There's no point in paying for two taxis.'

Tom's face fell and Cathy bit her lip. She wanted to be with Tom. Mavis would turn the excursion into an endurance test, but Cathy could not think of a polite way of refusing her.

'The museum? Could I tag along as well?'

This time it was Major O'Neill on the lookout for a free ride. Mavis glared at him. Apparently she had still not forgiven him for choosing to save Cathy from the kidnappers rather than looking after her. Cathy saw an opportunity.

'I'm afraid we are already taking this gentleman,' indicating her guard, 'so I'm afraid we haven't got room for both of you. Why don't the two of you share a taxi?'

She hurried towards the door, closely followed by Tom and the guard, leaving Mavis and the major confronting each other. Hastily she and Tom got in the back seat of the waiting taxi while the guard slid in beside the driver, and the vehicles set off while Cathy sighed with relief.

'They'll never forgive us,' she prophesied, 'but I couldn't have spent a morning with the two of them.'

'I don't care if they never speak to us again,' Tom said firmly. 'In fact, I'll be quite glad if they don't.'

He glanced out of the window. The taxi had turned off the main road and was speeding along a quiet side road. Tom leaned forward anxiously.

'We want to go to Luxor Museum,' he said to the driver.

The man nodded, and the taxi went even faster, scattering pedestrians.

'This is not the way to the museum!' Tom exclaimed, and tapped the bodyguard's shoulder. 'Tell him he is going the wrong way!'

The bodyguard turned round and smiled.

'He is going the right way as far as I am concerned.'

As Tom and Cathy stared at him in bewilderment he slipped his hand inside his jacket and drew out a small handgun.

'I am afraid your trip to the museum has been postponed indefinitely,' he said.

Cathy's first reaction was sheer disbelief, followed by fury. Tom made an abrupt movement, but stopped as the gun was lifted menacingly.

'If you attack me, I shall shoot,' the brown-suited man said calmly. 'I may hit you, or I may hit the lady. Either way, the car might crash. I suggest you sit quietly.'

Cathy clutched Tom's hand and closed her eyes. 'This can't be happening again! All I wanted was a quiet trip to a museum!'

The car drove through a network of back streets before swerving through a black gaping entrance where the driver stopped the car, leapt out and pulled together sliding doors which sealed off the outside world.

'Out now!' said the man with the gun, and Tom and Cathy scrambled out of the car and found themselves standing in a large empty space whose oil-stained concrete floor showed it had been a garage.

The gunman, with the driver beside him, surveyed his captives mockingly.

'That was very easy. In case you are worried, Inspector Hanif's man is safe in Miss Singleton's bathroom. However, he will not wake up for some time and then he will not have any useful information.' Tom went to speak but was silenced by a lifted hand. 'Yes, I know Inspector Hanif will make great efforts to find you, but Luxor is a large town.'

He gestured around him. 'This is a factory building which has been empty for some time. We are going to shut you away in a small, very secure room which was used for storing valuable materials. You will not be able to get out.'

'You're going to leave us to die!' Cathy burst out and he looked at her with irritation.

'Miss Singleton, if we wanted you dead I would have shot you both by now. All we intend to do is to keep you out of circulation for two or three days. If the inspector has not found you after three days, we will inform him where you are. We are businessmen and in the next forty-eight hours we intend to complete a very profitable business transaction. We are just making sure that neither of you interfere.'

'But we don't know who you are or what you intend to do!' Tom expostulated.

The gunman smiled disbelievingly. 'Of course you say that. It may be true, but we want to make quite sure.'

'Did Michael Anders interfere? He is in hospital fighting for his life.'

Now there was a scowl.

'Mr Anders would not have been hurt if he had not been very stupid. We had to make elaborate arrangements to ensure that you found him and could look after him.'

'You know that you are facing a lifetime in prison if you are caught. Is this business deal worth that? Why not just let us go? You could be long gone before we contact the police.'

'The profits will be worth the risk. Now we have talked enough.'

The gunman's attention had become focussed on Tom. Obviously he did not see Cathy as a threat. As for her, her sense of frustration and anger had been increasing steadily. The man might not intend to harm them, but she wanted to hurt him if she could! Now, as he gestured to the driver, she stepped forward and kicked him hard on the side of his knee. Thrown off balance, he gave a furious shout and toppled over, losing his grip on the gun.

Before he could reach for it Tom leaped forward, stamped on his fingers and scooped up the weapon. As the driver recovered from his surprise and began to move, Tom turned and punched him hard. The driver fell, hitting his head on the concrete floor with a thud, and lay motionless.

The gunman was on his knees now, but Tom hit him viciously with the gun and he fell to the floor. Tom grabbed Cathy's hand.

'Quick! They didn't lock the doors!'

It took five long seconds to open the door a crack big enough for them to squeeze through. Once outside, there was no-one around to see a wild-eyed Englishman clutching a gun in one hand and hauling a girl along with the other.

'There may be other members of the gang in the building,' Tom said tersely to Cathy. 'We've got to get where there are other people.'

They raced round one corner, then another, Tom remembering to tuck the gun in his pocket. There was a sprinkling of people now, and suddenly in the next street they were in the middle of a small market. Tom stopped and took a deep breath. Then he took out his mobile phone.

'Who are you calling?' Cathy asked. 'Magid or the ship?'

Tom looked at her grimly.

'Inspector Hanif.'

8

The room at the police station was small, but it did have two rather battered but comfortable chairs where Tom and Cathy could sip hibiscus tea while they waited for the inspector, which was fortunate as it was over an hour before Hanif finally appeared. He strode into the room and sat in the swivel chair, leant forward to put his elbows on the desk and rested his chin in his hands. To Cathy's surprise he looked calm, almost amused, as though he had gone past anger.

'The news so far,' he said. 'My man at the hotel was found unconscious in an empty room. Apparently he had been drugged but he is recovering. The two men and the car had left the factory which was, of course, empty when we searched it. However, we did find a small store room which had some bottles of water and biscuits in it. Presumably that is where you were supposed to spend the next three days. It would not have been pleasant. There was no light and very little fresh air.' He sat up straight. 'Mr Sanderson, Miss Singleton, it is time to tell me the whole truth.'

'I have!' Cathy said desperately. 'I don't know why these things keep happening to me.'

The inspector looked at her steadily but said nothing. After a minute of this Tom broke the silence.

'Miss Singleton is telling the truth. She works for a travel firm which sent her on this holiday to see if there was anything they should alter for their clients. Her cover story was rather thin and she was seen in the company of both myself and Michael Anders, so the kidnappers suspected that she was working with us.'

Inspector Hanif smiled like a cat stalking an unwary mouse. 'So if Miss Singleton has nothing to hide, will you tell me what you and Mr Anders were really doing in Egypt?'

Tom gave an exasperated sigh and rumpled his hair as Cathy stared at him.

'I suppose I'll have to, though there's not much to tell and I don't think it is going to help you much.'

The inspector sat back, watching Tom resolve his indecision.

'Well, first of all,' Tom began with a touch of defiance, 'I am here partly on holiday and partly on business. Everything I have told you is true. It's just that it wasn't quite the whole truth.'

Inspector Hanif waited. Tom fidgeted uneasily, then went on.

'A couple of weeks before I left, I was contacted by a friend of a friend and asked if I would help a certain international organisation by seeing if my business encounters would help me to find out anything about some matters in Egypt that were causing concern. It was thought that some of my contacts might help me get the information that was wanted. I'm not an agent or a spy, just a rank amateur who was asked to keep his eyes and ears open.'

'And Mr Anders?' interrupted Inspector Hanif.

'Ah, now he is very different. In fact, I suppose he is a spy, or a secret agent, whatever you like to call him. He works for a European government and a few months ago he was involved in some pretty rough stuff and was badly wounded.' Tom gave a mirthless grin. 'His employers thought a couple of weeks in Egypt would help him to convalesce, and at the same time he could liaise with me.'

Tom was silent for a few seconds. 'It didn't work out like that. We were supposed to find out what we could and pass the information back to the organisation, but that wasn't enough for Anders. When we linked up a couple of days after the cruise started I found he was desperate to prove to his employers that he had fully recovered and was determined to use this assignment to prove it. He wanted to take action.'

Tom looked at Cathy. 'That's why we were quarrelling when you saw us. Anders had found out certain facts which he wouldn't share with me because to him I was just an ignorant novice, but he told me that night that he was going to do something which would give him a whole lot more information. I said we weren't supposed to take risks and he called me a coward. That was the last time I saw him.'

Inspector Hanif was looking grim. 'Egypt is my country. If something illegal is taking place here, then it is for me to investigate, not outsiders.'

Tom nodded wearily. 'I understand how you feel. But this crime is international. Your government is working with the organisation that contacted me, and when there is evidence enough then it is your police force which will act on it.'

'What crime are you talking about?' Cathy interrupted impatiently.

'Theft. Theft of Egyptian antiquities. Every country suffers from art thieves who sell off their countries' treasures to the highest bidder. Galleries, museums, stately homes — all have been the victims of such theft though international co-operation does recover much of the booty eventually. But Egypt is a special case. There are many undiscovered treasures buried here. If objects are found in illegal excavations and smuggled abroad, no one even knows a theft has taken place.'

'Fantastic treasures can vanish into private collections and never be recorded. Just think of the worldwide sensation when Tutankhamun's tomb was found, yet he was a minor pharaoh buried in a hurry in a small tomb. To the thieves and smugglers the objects they sell are just sources of money, yet the real problem is that every time they break into a grave and disperse its contents they are destroying a part of Egypt's heritage, an unknown part of its history.'

He was speaking with real feeling,

and Cathy recalled his appreciation of the antiquities they had seen. Frustrating criminals who were stealing the historic artefacts of Egypt would give him great personal satisfaction. No wonder he had agreed to help track down such thieves!

Inspector Hanif's posture had changed slightly. He had stopped leaning forward almost threateningly. The interrogation had become a discussion.

'Everything you say is true, of course. We have managed to reduce the illegal trade in antiquities, but we know that each year some objects are spirited out of Egypt. There are dealers who promise peasants ready money for anything they find, and that is a great temptation for a poor man.'

Now Tom was leaning forward.

'But from the rumours Anders and I have heard, this isn't a matter of a few pots or some scraps of papyrus. This is something big!'

'Do you mean that someone has found a tomb? An important tomb?'

Tom nodded eagerly. 'The word is that it isn't a royal tomb, but it is obviously the tomb of an important government official, probably about the time of Rameses the Second. The story is that it was discovered about a year ago by a farmer. He kept quiet about it because he didn't want strangers plundering the tomb, but he couldn't resist dropping hints to his family and one or two close friends, though he wouldn't give any details. A gang of smugglers heard about it, its members came to investigate, and for the past year the gang has been working in great secrecy to remove the tomb's contents and arrange to get them abroad.'

'Why didn't you come to us?' Hanif expostulated.

'Because we had no proof. We felt we needed some evidence we could bring to you. You know how each year there are rumours that some splendid tomb has been discovered, only for the story to be disproved as wishful thinking. You might have thought that this was just another fantasy.'

'Why do you think these rumours are different?' Cathy asked.

The two men almost jumped. She got the impression they had quite forgotten she was there.

'A couple of things,' Tom told her. 'For one thing, the farmer who was supposed to have located the tomb disappeared soon afterwards and nobody has been able to find any trace of him. For another, the international organisation has noticed unusual financial transactions by some of the world's richest and most unscrupulous collectors. Property and investments are being turned into cash.'

'Imagine what would happen if the contents of a rich tomb were smuggled out of Egypt and the details were circulated. There would be the most amazing worldwide secret auction. Think of it! The complete contents of an ancient Egypt tomb! Bidding would be in millions, possibly billions, and the buyer would have to be able to pay quickly and secretly.' He glanced apologetically at the inspector. 'But it still wasn't really enough to approach you.'

The inspector was looking thoughtful.

'Sometimes gut feelings are as convincing as hard evidence, and in this case, even if the possibility of an important tomb having been found is remote, I think we should act as if the rumours were true. Better safe than sorry.'

He pulled a pad of paper towards him with a business-like air. 'First of all, we shall check the current whereabouts and activities of known smugglers and dealers willing to take part in illegal trading. Then we will try to locate anybody suspicious who seems to have disappeared within the last few months.' He looked at Tom and Cathy. 'Thirdly, we must try and find out quickly which member of your party is also a member of the gang.'

Cathy sat up abruptly when she saw Tom nodding agreement.

'Are you suggesting that someone in

our group, one of the holidaymakers, is a criminal?'

'One of them must be,' Tom said a little impatiently. 'Otherwise how could they have kept watch on us and been able to plan our abduction?'

Cathy gulped, thinking of Mrs Redcar and Mavis, the major and the much-travelled married couple. None of them seemed likely suspects.

'I did make a list,' Tom said. 'I was trying to work out who it was most likely to be. If we can use the information you have on file about smugglers and dealers we may be able to identify the man — or woman.'

'It will take me some time to get these searches done,' Hanif told him. 'It will probably be tomorrow morning before we can take any action. To avoid giving the guilty person any hint of what we are doing, I suggest you and Miss Singleton continue to behave like normal tourists. You were trying to reach Luxor Museum when you were abducted? May I suggest that you go there now. I will make sure that your taxi-driver can be trusted!'

Cathy could not believe her ears. She had been kidnapped and held at gunpoint, informed that she might have made friends with a criminal who was planning one of the greatest robberies the world had ever known, and now she was expected to visit a museum!

To her surprise, however, Tom apparently thought it a good idea, pointing out that they must try to avoid making the gang member suspicious.

The museum was modern and well laid-out, but Cathy could scarcely spare the exhibits a glance.

'How can you concentrate on these?' she demanded, waving a hand at the carefully-lit displays. 'We have been in danger — real danger. There are international criminals out to get us!'

Tom stopped examining an elegant daybed, took her by the arm and led her to a seat.

'What else do you suggest we do? Go back to the hotel and lock ourselves in our rooms? This whole situation has only arisen because people covet the beautiful things that Egyptians have produced. Now you are being given a chance, and it may be your only chance, to look at some of the finest works the ancient Egyptians ever produced. If you can't appreciate them, just sit here and let me enjoy them.'

Subdued, Cathy followed him back to the exhibits. After a while he unbent enough to start giving her information about the objects and their history, until she found herself sharing his enthusiasm. By the time they had finished the tour, she was very glad they had come.

'I want that black statue,' she said covetously. 'You know, the king with his fists clenched.'

'I know the one. It is magnificent. Do you realise that a couple of thousand years ago the priests decided it was out of date and buried it in a hole in the ground?'

'At least in Egypt things which are

buried usually stay in good condition.' Her eyes widened. 'Do you think there could be things like these in this mysterious tomb?'

'Lower your voice!' Tom said sharply, and then nodded. 'It's possible, and that's why we don't want such treasures vanishing into somebody's private collection when they could give pleasure to millions.'

When they returned to the hotel it was difficult to accept that everything seemed perfectly normal, that people could be debating where to have dinner rather than speculating on who were the criminals in their midst.

Mrs Redcar, sitting in the lounge with Major O'Neill, was one of the first to see them and she beckoned them over.

'It's taken you a long time to visit the museum. I thought you would be back for lunch.'

Tom signalled to a waiter and ordered tea while Cathy sank down beside her friend.

'It was marvellous,' she said sincerely,

'but after we'd been there we decided to have lunch by the Nile and then . . . ' She hesitated and gave Tom a pleading look as her imagination failed her.

'And then we went for a carriage drive and another look at Karnak,' he said smoothly. 'What have you been doing?'

'Reading, sunbathing and chatting. Very restful. Tomorrow I shall indulge in a little more culture.' Mrs Redcar rose and gathered up her bag and book. 'I shall see you at dinner, Major.' She strode away and the major excused himself soon afterwards. They saw him making for the bar, presumably in the hope that someone would be willing to buy him a drink.

Tom looked at his watch. 'There are still a couple of hours before dinner. Why don't you go and have a rest in your room?'

'What are you going to do?' Cathy said suspiciously. 'If you are going to call Inspector Hanif, I want to know what he says.'

Tom looked at her with exasperation. 'He'll call us if he finds out anything interesting. I am going to have a rest and a long shower, because I feel as tired as you look.'

The day's events were a dramatic jumble in her whirling brain, but she found herself concentrating on the puzzle of which one of her holiday companions was part of the smuggling gang. It had to be someone familiar with Egypt, someone intelligent who had kept a close eye on Cathy and Tom. Slowly she realised that one person fitted the description perfectly. Mrs Redcar!

Mrs Redcar had kept close to Cathy all their time in Egypt, questioning her about her real motives for coming on the cruise, asking her about Tom and assuming the two of them were close. It had to be Mrs Redcar!

Cathy was very quiet at dinner that night, letting her table companions assume that she was still tired from the day's activities. Mavis dominated the conversation with stories of the bargains she had bought in the market, with emphasis on her bargaining skills.

'You might have done even better if you could speak the language, like Mrs Redcar,' one man observed, and while Mavis disputed this Cathy realised that this was one more pointer to Mrs Redcar's guilt.

After dinner she drew Tom into the privacy of the garden and told him her suspicions. He was first amused and then scornful.

'She's scarcely my idea of a criminal.'

'That's precisely why she is likely to be one!' She clenched her fists as he smiled disbelievingly. 'At least call Inspector Hanif and tell him what I think.'

Finally he agreed to do so, probably just to keep her quiet, she suspected, and they drifted back into the hotel.

9

The end of the holiday was approaching, and in the lounge the after-dinner conversation was about the best souvenirs to take home and how much they should tip the hotel staff. Mavis was announcing that she never tipped the staff on principle when the door was suddenly flung wide and Inspector Hanif strode in, followed by two policemen. Without hesitation he made straight for Mrs Redcar and came to a halt in front of her.

'Mrs Redcar? Mrs Amelia Redcar?'

She looked up in surprise and gave a slight nod.

'Will you come with me, please?'

It was Mavis who leant forward and demanded shrilly. 'What do you want to see her about?'

Inspector Hanif ignored her and waited. Mrs Redcar stood up and hooked her bag over her arm.

'Don't worry, Mavis. I've probably forgotten to fill in some form.' She turned to the inspector. 'I hope this won't take long.' Then, preceded by the inspector and with the two policemen following her closely, she went out of the lounge.

Immediately there was a buzz of speculation, though Cathy did not join in. She was feeling guilty, in a strange kind of way. After all, Mrs Redcar had been kind to her.

Half an hour passed and Mrs Redcar had not returned. All eyes turned to the door when it finally opened, but it was one of the policemen who entered and politely informed Tom and Cathy that the inspector would be grateful for a word with them.

They could hear the voices raised behind them in excitement before the door had even closed.

The policeman led them to the small office which Hanif had used before, and when they went in they saw the inspector and Mrs Redcar seated side by side, laughing like old friends, with coffee on the table in front of them.

'Come in!' said the inspector, leaping up. 'Hassan, more coffee for our guests.'

'Mrs Redcar . . . ' Cathy said, taking a chair while nervously eyeing the older woman.

'Mrs Redcar is helping me with my enquiries,' Hanif said cheerfully, and his companion laughed aloud.

'Relax, my dear. Did you really think I was a member of an international gang of smugglers? I'm flattered!'

The inspector looked at Cathy indulgently. 'Mrs Redcar and I have met before. After all, her husband was an important official at the British Embassy for several years. That is when she learnt to speak Arabic.'

Cathy was blushing hotly, aware of Tom glaring at her reproachfully. 'Then why did you come and take her away so abruptly? It looked as if you were arresting her.'

'That was the impression I was trying

to give, so that the real criminal would relax her guard and give me some extra time to search for more evidence.'

Cathy's coffee cup splashed back on the saucer. 'Her? But the only other woman is Mavis!'

Mrs Redcar and Inspector Hanif nodded in unison.

'Mavis,' said Mrs Redcar. 'Mavis who tried to stop Major O'Neill rescuing you at the temple, who sent you and Tom to the house where you were held captive, who tried to get into the taxi with the fake bodyguard when you were going to the museum. Mavis, who was heard speaking fluent Arabic in the market this morning.'

'Mavis,' took up the inspector, 'who had letters in her room from various dealers who want to see the treasures she is bringing out of Egypt. She also had duplicate keys to some rooms and safes.'

'So what happens now?' Tom enquired, once they had recovered from their first disbelief.

'Now it is your turn to help. Will you please go back to the lounge, tell everybody that I was asking you questions about Mrs Redcar, and that you think she has been arrested. Keep Mavis talking so that she stays there for a while longer.'

Obediently Cathy and Tom left the inspector and Mrs Redcar in the office and crossed the reception area. Tom held the lounge door open for Cathy to enter and both of them looked at the corner where Mavis had been sitting. Major O'Neill was there but Mavis had disappeared.

'Mavis went out soon after the police took you away. I expect she was trying to find out what was happening. You know how inquisitive she is.'

'And she never came back?'

Major O'Neill was frowning.

'No. But she could have gone up to her room, I suppose. Why? Does it matter?'

'It matters because our Mavis may be trying to escape from the police!' Cathy snapped.

Tom gave her an angry look.

'Miss Singleton is being rather too dramatic,' he said coldly. 'However, we do need to find Mavis as soon as possible.'

The Major was on his feet; eager to show he was a man of action. 'Let me help.'

The Egyptian policemen, notified of what had happened, joined in the search, but Mavis was not in her room. Nor was she in the restaurant, the little boutiques or the beauty salon. Growing desperate, Cathy even checked that she was not in the gymnasium.

'Where can she be?' she appealed to Tom. 'The police are guarding the front entrance to the hotel.'

He stood thinking, hands on hips, and then his head lifted sharply. 'We've overlooked the obvious. Perhaps she is trying to escape across the Nile. An accomplice could come to the edge of the hotel gardens in a small boat.'

They hurried through the building out into the gardens. At this time of night just a few lights glimmered near the hotel. Near the river's bank there was darkness amid the shrubbery, and Tom plunged into the shadows. Then Cathy froze as she heard the sound of an outboard motor near the bank.

'There's a boat coming!' she shouted.

Somebody in the hotel sprang into action and suddenly all the lights in the garden were switched on, so that every detail of the gardens was harshly floodlit. Major O'Neill gave a triumphant shout.

'There she is!'

Mavis's slight form was running for the riverbank and the safety of the boat, but Tom was close behind her. Abruptly Mavis stopped, swung round and faced her pursuer. Something gleamed in her hand.

'She's got a gun!' Cathy screamed. The Major sprinted past her, but he could not reach Mavis in time. As the woman brought her gun up, focussing on Tom, Cathy looked around desperately, picked up a glass tankard abandoned on a table and threw it as hard as she could. It hit Mavis on the head and the gun dropped from her hand. She seemed to fold up, dropping to the ground just as Major O'Neill pounced on her.

Within seconds an Egyptian policeman had handcuffed a dazed Mavis, while somewhere below them the boat turned and accelerated away into the darkness. Then the police arrived in force and Mavis was rapidly driven away. Inspector Hanif found Tom with his arms round Cathy, trying to reassure her that all was well now.

'What happens now?' Cathy managed to ask.

'Now I contact a large number of people and then we interrogate the lady. I suggest you two get a good night's sleep.'

Cathy stared after him indignantly. 'He can't just leave us like that! I want to know what happens next.'

'I expect we'll find out eventually,' Tom said comfortingly. 'But there's no room for amateurs at the moment.' He looked up. 'Anyway, here's Mrs Redcar come to look after you.'

Mrs Redcar quietly but firmly saw Cathy to her room, where she sat her down and demanded to know the full story.

Cathy spent the next half hour telling Mrs Redcar the whole saga, from the moment her holiday plans were so drastically changed to the moment it was realised that Mavis was a member of a criminal gang. Mrs Redcar listened attentively and made no comments till Cathy had finished. Then she sighed wistfully.

'I wish it had been me! I haven't had any adventures for years!'

'Well I don't want any more!' Cathy said firmly. 'From now on I am going to lead a dull, quiet life.' She hesitated. 'But I do want to know how the story finishes.'

'Maybe we shall hear something tomorrow,' said Mrs Redcar. 'Meanwhile, get a good night's sleep.'

In fact Cathy got a few hours' sleep before she was rudely awakened by an urgent knocking on the door. Stumbling across the room, opening the door a crack, she found Tom outside.

'They know where the tomb is!' were his first words. 'Mavis won't say a word, but Michael Anders is recovering, thank heavens, and he had got enough scraps of information for the police to locate it. Archaeologists have been flying in all night!'

'Marvellous!' said Cathy, still half asleep, but this wasn't enough for Tom.

'Well? Don't you want to see it? There is a car waiting for us downstairs. You've got five minutes to dress.'

Cathy just made it, and the car roared off into the Egyptian night and across the Nile. It finally joined a cluster of vehicles in a sandstone gully, where a group was examining an apparently solid rock face. Soon there was a cry of triumph as sand was scooped away to reveal a narrow crevice. Tom pressed forward, clasping

Cathy's hand, and she found herself descending a steep, narrow flight of steps.

At the bottom, powerful lanterns were already illuminating a chamber whose walls were decorated with elaborate paintings. Unlike the tombs of the Valley Of The Kings, these did not portray gods. Instead fathers played with their children, went fishing, and embraced their wives.

'This is beautiful!' somebody breathed. 'This is high-class work in perfect condition.'

But the floor of the tomb was bare apart from a few shards of broken pottery. Every article it contained had been removed. Cathy turned to Tom.

'Surely Mavis will have to say where the contents are?'

Tom shrugged. 'It's going to be difficult to prove she was anything more than a go-between for the robbers and the would-be buyers. If the grave goods can still be smuggled out of the country they can still be sold. I think Mavis feels that a year or so in prison might be worth it if she can come out and find a fortune waiting for her as a reward for her silence.'

'Where are they likely to be hidden?'

'Anywhere. In a house or a factory, buried underground or in containers in some lorry park. There is going to be an intensive search, of course, but it will be sheer luck if the goods are found.'

This was depressing, frustrating news. They were taken back to their hotel but Cathy could not go back to sleep. She lay on her bed, her mind racing. Somehow the grave goods had to be found!

She frowned irritably as she heard the occupants of the next room get up, open and shut drawers and the irritating noise penetrated the wall. Then she sat up slowly. There was something about a wall, something which she should remember. Then it came back to her and she was off her bed in a flash, pushing her feet into her sandals. She raced along the corridors, thumping first on Tom's door and then on Mrs Redcar's.

'I've got an idea!' she told them. 'I want to see Inspector Hanif.'

A short taxi-ride later and she and her friends were ushered into the office where the inspector sat talking into the telephone, dark shadows under his eyes betraying the fact that he had worked through the night. He finished his conversation and put the telephone down.

'I may be wrong,' Cathy said without preamble, 'but it's worth checking. When we were kidnapped Tom was tapping the walls, looking for a way out. One wall sounded hollow and we thought the cellar of the neighbouring house must be on the other side. But when we got out we could see that the house was standing on its own.'

The inspector was on his feet, beckoning a subordinate. 'We will check. I'll go there at once.'

'We'll go there,' Cathy said firmly. 'We've earned the right, I think.'

Somehow the weary man summoned

up a smile. 'I think you have as well, though I warn you I may lose my temper if this is a wild-goose chase.'

In the end it was over an hour before a caravan of cars had been assembled containing Cathy, Tom, the inspector and assorted policemen, together with archaeologists and various workmen clutching tools that might be useful. The journey through Luxor and over the Nile was comparatively short, but they noticed the inspector peering behind them as if expecting other cars to follow.

'I am looking out for the media — papers and television,' Hanif told them. 'There are sure to have been some leaks during the past hours, and everyone will soon be eager to get any details of the treasure hunt.'

'If there is nothing there, I am going to look an absolute fool,' muttered Cathy despairingly.

Tom patted her knee comfortingly. 'Just think what a heroine you will be if there is something.'

The house was empty when they reached it. Cathy hesitated at the door, remembering the claustrophobia and fear she had felt in the cellar, but then she lifted her chin and strode in and down the stairs, closely followed by Tom.

Once in the cellar, he stood frowning with his hands on his hips for a few seconds and then went confidently to a section of the wall and rapped on it. There was a hollow sound, and immediately two well-built men in overalls advanced, one armed with a sledgehammer and the other carrying a pickaxe.

There were a few heavy blows before the wall cracked and pieces of plaster fell from it. These were picked away and a hole about a foot square could be seen. Inspector Hanif gestured to the men to stand aside and approached the wall, carrying a torch, which he shone through into the darkness beyond.

Cathy remembered what Tom had told her, that when Howard Carter had shone the first light in over three

thousand years on Tutankhamun's treasure he had been dazzled by the gleam
of gold. She craned forward expectantly.

Inspector Hanif turned round, his
expression enigmatic.

'What is there?' Cathy demanded.

'Boxes, Miss Singleton. Cardboard
boxes and wooden crates.' He turned
back to the two men, snapping out a
few words, and carefully they began to
enlarge the hole till everybody could see
the packing cases piled behind the wall.
Two of the archaeologists came forward
as the hole grew.

They stepped over the crumbled
plaster and very carefully cut the tape
fastening one box, then opened the box
and drew out a bundle wrapped in
crumpled newspapers. These they removed, revealing white tissue paper, which
was removed with gentle hands, finally
revealing an exquisite alabaster jar. The
two archaeologists looked at it closely,
twisting it this way and that, before they
looked up with expressions of triumph
and relief.

'This came from the tomb,' one said. 'The hieroglyphics prove it.'

Inspector Hanif broke the silence. 'Now, if you please, I want everybody except the archaeologists and their helpers to leave so that there is room for them to work. We must let the experts find out exactly what we have here.'

'They aren't going to unpack everything quickly just to see what there is. They will take weeks, possibly months, identifying and recording every object before it is moved from that cellar. But you were right, my dear, and Egypt is going to be very grateful to you,' said Inspector Hanif comfortingly.

So, once again, it was back to the hotel. Cathy and Tom had a celebratory breakfast-cum-lunch, together with Mrs Redcar when she had been told the news. Major O'Neill was also present, invited by Mrs Redcar on the grounds that after all he was the one who had actually, physically, caught Mavis.

'This has definitely been my most

exciting Nile cruise so far,' Mrs Redcar announced. 'And to think that at this time tomorrow we will be on an aeroplane flying back to England, where the forecast is heavy rain.'

Cathy sat up. 'Going back? Tomorrow?' She groaned, mentally counting the days. 'I'd completely lost track of time.'

She thought of the careful list of notes she had made for Mr Hunter during the first few days. It had been abandoned for some time. She would have to find an hour or so to complete it, but it would seem a very dull occupation after what had happened.

Later Tom saw Cathy to her room after she announced that she was going to sleep for at least twelve hours.

'Today was worth all we went through, wasn't it?'

She smiled up at him. 'It has been a marvellous holiday. I can't wait to get home and tell my parents all about it. My mother was worried about me getting a tummy bug. Wait till she hears that I was kidnapped by a gang of international criminals!'

'Other girls would have had screaming hysterics. I'm glad I met you, Cathy Singleton.'

With that he leant forward, kissed her light on the forehead, and then swung round and walked away rapidly before she could say a word. Well, at least they would be able to spend the last day together.

10

The next morning Cathy started to pack before going down to breakfast, though she found it difficult to accept that this was really to be her last day in Egypt. She was just enjoying a final cup of coffee when a waiter murmured discreetly that Inspector Hanif would like to see her when she had finished — there was no hurry. However her curiosity was strong and she abandoned her half-full cup and hurried to the little office where the inspector was waiting.

Inspector Hanif looked fresh and full of energy. He had obviously enjoyed a good night's sleep and smiled as he came forward to greet her.

'Miss Singleton! I bring you the heartfelt gratitude and thanks of the Egyptian police and archaeologists. I also came to bring you up to date with the latest news before you return home.

Please sit down.'

A tray of coffee was brought and when the ritual of pouring it out had been completed, the inspector began.

'First of all, as you witnessed, the contents of the cellar did come from the empty tomb, and the man who was buried there was a high official under Rameses the Second. Historically, as well as in terms of treasure trove, this is a very important discovery. A statement has been issued saying merely that a tomb and its contents have been found but there will be public reference to the smugglers' activities.'

'Secondly, there is the problem of Mavis Elton, who refuses to say anything except demand the protection of the British officials, who are highly embarrassed by her activities. It has been decided that putting an elderly lady on trial would be very bad publicity, especially as we are not sure she could be convicted of any major crime. The way she deceived everybody shows what a superb actress she is, and she could put on quite a show in court.'

'Therefore it has been decided that she will be deported today, and it will be made very clear to her that the police will be keeping an eye on her in the future in case she is tempted to indulge in any similar behaviour. Finally, you will be pleased to know that Michael Anders is making good progress, and although he exceeded his instructions I think his employers will feel that the result excused his over-zealous behaviour.'

'When the grave goods are displayed eventually it will be one of the most outstanding events in Egyptology for some decades, and I will make sure that you and Mr Sanderson, and my friend, Mrs Redcar, will all be invited to inspect it as guests of the Egyptian government.'

'You will probably also be pleased to hear that we have arrested the two men who took you to the factory yesterday. One of them made a call to Mavis Elton, presumably to warn her that you had escaped, and we traced the call and found them.'

He sat back, smiling.

'Thank you for taking the time to come and tell me this,' Cathy said gratefully. 'I'm glad I did help, though I only got involved in things accidentally, unlike Mr Sanderson.' She looked round. 'Where is he, by the way? Don't say he is still asleep!'

Inspector Hanif looked at her in surprise.

'Don't you know? Mr Sanderson checked out of the hotel early this morning.'

★   ★   ★

Later Cathy threw her remaining clothes in her suitcase and slammed the lid down viciously. How dare Tom leave without saying goodbye to her? It was his fault that she had been kidnapped and threatened, and he hadn't even apologised. And how many times had he kissed her? Did that mean nothing?

Mrs Redcar, when interrogated, had disclaimed all knowledge of why he had gone so early without even leaving a message.

'Perhaps he had an urgent business appointment,' was all she could say.

Cathy slumped down in the chair. Not only was she furious with Tom, but also there was a strong feeling of anti-climax about the day anyway. The coach would take them to the airport in the early evening, and until then there was nothing to do but wander through Luxor and the hotel or look for last-minute presents.

Resignedly she finished her packing and then picked up her handbag. She was not going to spend her last hours in Egypt sulking in her room. She would go out and try to enjoy her last day.

It wasn't too bad. She bought some attractive small presents for her parents, and even bought a glass perfume bottle for her friend, Mary. After all, if Mary hadn't chosen to go to Majorca with her boyfriend, Cathy would never have come to Egypt.

Shopping done, she sauntered along

the promenade by the side of the Nile, admiring the elegant feluccas as they glided along the river. Now, what else could she do?

'Miss Singleton!' said a pleased voice. It was Major O'Neill, looking very dapper in his newly-mended blazer. 'I hope you are enjoying your last day.'

'Very much, thank you,' Cathy said politely.

'Would you like a cup of coffee? There's a very pleasant café just there with a good view of the river.'

Cathy could not think of an excuse, and anyway she had been thinking it was time for a rest, so the two of them settled into the café.

'It is a marvellous view, isn't it?' Major O'Neill said a little wistfully, gazing at the river. 'Each time I come here I tell myself it is for the last time, but after a while I want to come again.'

'So you'll probably be back here in the future?'

The major looked despondent. 'I don't know. I think this may indeed prove to be the last time.'

Cathy remembered Mrs Redcar's theory that the major lived in genteel poverty and Tom's belief that times were getting harder for him. She, in turn, looked at the river. Tomorrow she would be back in rainy England and a couple of days later she would be behind her desk in the travel agency.

Major O'Neill chattered on, with Cathy occasionally contributing a brief reply, but finally she decided it was time to go back to the hotel and add the presents she had bought to her luggage. She started to push her chair back and the major took the hint.

'Time we were off? I'll just pay for the coffees.' Confidently he put his hand in his pocket, frowned, and tried another pocket. There was consternation on his face.

'I don't seem to have my wallet with me. I must have left it in my room.'

He waited expectantly. 'What a pity,' she said placidly, waiting to see what he would say next.

He gave an embarrassed little cough. 'Do you think — could you possibly pay the bill, Miss Singleton? I'll pay you back at the hotel.'

Suddenly all Cathy's bad temper, made worse by her disappointment over Tom, rose to the surface. She was not going to be another of Major O'Neill's victims! She smiled sweetly.

'I'm afraid I haven't any money left. Now, if you'll excuse me, I really must go. Thank you for the coffee.'

She stood up and walked rapidly away, looking over her shoulder once in time to see him in hot debate with the waiter.

Cathy hadn't gone fifty yards before remorse overcame her. Why hadn't she just offered to pay? After all, he had rescued her from that first attempted abduction, and he had helped capture Mavis. He deserved gratitude, not being put in an embarrassing situation. She hesitated, stopped walking and decided she ought to go back, but at that moment Cathy saw Mrs Redcar coming towards her. The older woman saw at once that something was wrong.

'What's the matter?'

'I've been thoroughly mean to Major O'Neill, and now I'll have to go back and try to sort it out.'

She explained briefly and Mrs Redcar frowned. 'If you go back, he'll know you thought he was lying about his wallet. I'll deal with it.'

Feeling she had escaped lightly from an awkward situation, Cathy went back to the hotel and finished packing. Neither the major nor Mrs Redcar appeared at lunch, for which she was grateful, and afterwards she decided to spend a final hour relaxing in the gardens beside the Nile. Relaxation turned into a gentle doze, but she woke with a jump when somebody sat down beside her and gave a significant cough. It was Mrs Redcar.

'I just thought you should know what happened this morning,' she announced. 'I went in the café, where Major O'Neill was still trying to deal with the situation, and I offered to pay immediately I was told what the problem was. Then the Major and I had another coffee and a long talk.' She stopped, and for once looked a little unsure of herself. 'Well, the upshot of the talk was — that the Major and I are going to be married,' she ended in a rush.

Cathy sat bolt upright and stared at her.

'You are going to marry Major O'Neill?' she asked incredulously.

Mrs Redcar looked defiant. 'I like him,' she said simply. 'He is a very pleasant man, charming and well-mannered. All he needs is a little extra money so that he can live the life he wants to live. Well, I've plenty of money, so there's no problem there.' She smiled appealingly. 'We have enjoyed each other's company these last few days. We are two lonely people who can give each other companionship and affection.'

They looked at each other and Cathy stretched out her hand.

'Then I congratulate you, both of

you, and I know you will be happy.'

'Thank you.' Mrs Redcar rose. 'I left him waiting inside while I told you.' For a moment the familiar steely look returned. 'And incidentally, Major O'Neill has assured me that he did leave his wallet at the hotel.'

Soon the relentless routine of a holiday rapidly ending came into play. Luggage was collected, coaches toured the hotels picking up clients and then returned towards the airport.

Cathy waited in the departure lounge with Mrs Redcar and Major O'Neill for their flight to be called and observed the way they held hands and the Major's look of dazed happiness. She was sure that they would do very well together. Mrs Redcar would organise their lives very efficiently and Cathy could imagine the pleasures they would take in travelling the world. She had already exchanged addresses with Mrs Redcar and been assured that she would be invited to the wedding.

'And of course we will meet when the

Egyptian tomb's grave goods go on display,' she was reminded. 'That will be a big event.'

Back in England, Cathy's parents would be waiting for her and it would, as forecast, be raining.

Her parents would be full of questions, and Cathy found that while she would have no difficulty telling them all about the temples, the boat and Luxor, she was not sure how she could break the news that she had been kidnapped — twice — escaped from a gang of dangerous criminals and helped to discover a priceless treasure. She told herself that she did not want to overwhelm them with the news immediately and would break the details of her adventures to them gradually over the next few days.

On Monday she would return to work and give John Hunter her short list of notes about minor improvements which could be made to the Nile cruises, and then she would be immersed in her usual routine. She would soon forget the man who had brought excitement and adventure into her life but had not cared enough about her to even say goodbye.

They moved from the departure lounge to the designated gate and finally into the aeroplane. Once again there was an empty seat beside Cathy. Presumably it had been intended for Tom Sanderson.

The plane's engine grew louder as it prepared for takeoff and Cathy tensed involuntarily and closed her eyes. There was sudden movement next to her.

'Here, take my hand,' said a familiar voice. It was Tom Sanderson.

She stared at him unbelievingly. 'I thought you had gone. You checked out and you didn't even say goodbye.'

'Last night two policemen woke me at one in the morning, saying Michael Anders wanted to see me urgently. I threw my things into my case and checked out because they told me they didn't know how long I would be. At the hospital Anders said he had started to remember other things he had found out, about other smugglers and their activities. He wanted us to put all the information we had together before I flew back to England.'

'We went over everything we had learned, with the result that early in the morning I was in a very uncomfortable Land Rover bumping over desolate bits of desert and through tiny villages. I have spent the whole day helping to identify places where smuggling might be taking place. Finally I was driven straight to the airport. I thought I would arrive just in time to see your plane take off.'

Cathy was biting her lip. 'I thought you couldn't even be bothered to say goodbye, that I was just someone who'd accidentally got mixed up in your affairs, and that you wanted to forget me as soon as everything was sorted out.'

'I'm sorry you thought that. I was afraid you would decide I was nothing but trouble and that you would be glad I had gone.' He paused. 'If I had missed the plane, I would have come to see you in England.'

She avoided his eyes. They were going home and it was time to be sensible.

'We might not have liked each other when we met again. These adventures in Egypt haven't given us a chance to get to know each other properly. It was strange and exciting, but it wasn't normal life.'

'Then we need to be together a lot so that we can get to know each other properly,' he said firmly.

Her heart leapt. Being sensible stopped being so important.

Looking past Tom, she saw Mrs Redcar and Major O'Neill openly peering at them with interest.

'We thought you had vanished for ever, Mr Sanderson.'

'Just slightly delayed, Mrs Redcar.'

'Congratulate them!' Cathy whispered urgently. 'They are going to be married.'

Tom's eyebrows rose and he beckoned the steward.

'A bottle of champagne, please,' he requested. 'The four of us want to toast the future.'

THE END

We do hope that you have enjoyed reading this large print book.

Did you know that all of our titles are available for purchase?

We publish a wide range of high quality large print books including:
Romances, Mysteries, Classics
General Fiction
Non Fiction and Westerns

Special interest titles available in large print are:
The Little Oxford Dictionary
Music Book, Song Book
Hymn Book, Service Book

Also available from us courtesy of Oxford University Press:
Young Readers' Dictionary
(large print edition)
Young Readers' Thesaurus
(large print edition)

For further information or a free brochure, please contact us at:
Ulverscroft Large Print Books Ltd.,
The Green, Bradgate Road, Anstey,
Leicester, LE7 7FU, England.
Tel: (00 44) **0116 236 4325**
Fax: (00 44) **0116 234 0205**

A FRAGILE SANCTUARY

Roberta Grieve

When Jess Fenton refuses to have her disabled sister locked away, her employer turns them out of their cottage. Wandering the country lanes in search of work, they find unlikely sanctuary at a privately run home for the mentally ill — the very place that Jess had vowed her sister would never enter. As she settles into her new job, Jess finds herself falling in love with the owner of Chalfont Hall, even as she questions his motivation in running such a place.

SHIFTING SANDS

Shelagh Fenton

Ruth's father tells her that he has taken on Paul as a business partner, and whilst being obliged to co-operate with him, Ruth's reaction is to feel a deep distrust for a man she hardly knows. However, she comes to trust him and love him as they work together to track down her cousin Melanie, who has disappeared. Then Paul saves Ruth's life at serious cost to himself . . . just as they finally locate Melanie who is in great danger . . .

ONCE UPON A TIME

Zelma Falkiner

City girl Meredith plans to write a novel in the peace and quiet of the country, but finds her chosen retreat is over-run by a film production company. Despite her best intentions, she is soon lured from her story-telling into a make-believe world of early Australia, with handsome, bearded bush-rangers on horseback, and women in long skirts, boots and gingham bonnets. But in the real world, a little girl is in danger . . .

A TOUCH OF MAGIC

June Gadsby

Lorna is trying to rebuild her life after the war that robbed her of her husband and her son of a father he never knew. However, eleven-year-old Simon refuses to accept that Max is dead. Lorna does not believe in miracles, but it is Christmas and all Simon asks is the chance to see the place where his father's plane crashed. In the dense Basque forest, a man called Olentzero brings a touch of magic back into their lives . . .

A DREAM COME TRUE

Chrissie Loveday

Jess inherits an idyllic cottage in Cornwall and is determined to begin a new life. But there are surprises waiting. Someone is entering the cottage each time she goes out. Are they hoping to drive her away? If so, why? Can she risk abandoning everything she knows to move away from her parents? Dan, her new neighbour, and his family are persuasive — and she could see a future for herself in Cornwall . . . if she can get over the problems.